Edward Field

Esek Hopkins, commander-in-chief of the continental navy during

the American revolution

1775 to 1778

Edward Field

Esek Hopkins, commander-in-chief of the continental navy during the American revolution
1775 to 1778

ISBN/EAN: 9783337133900

Printed in Europe, USA, Canada, Australia, Japan

Cover: Foto ©Raphael Reischuk / pixelio.de

More available books at **www.hansebooks.com**

ESEK HOPKINS

BOOKS BY EDWARD FIELD.

Tax Lists of the Town of Providence during the Administration of Sir Edmund Andros. 1686-1689.

Sq. 8vo. $1.00 net.

Revolutionary Defences in Rhode Island.

WITH MAPS, PLANS, AND ILLUSTRATIONS
8vo. $2.25 net.

The Colonial Tavern: A Glimpse of New England Town Life in the Seventeenth and Eighteenth Centuries.

8vo. $2.00 net.

Esek Hopkins: Commander-In-Chief of the Continental Navy during the American Revolution, 1775 to 1778.

ILLUSTRATED. 8vo. $3.00 net.

ESEK HOPKINS

COMMANDER-IN-CHIEF

OF

THE CONTINENTAL NAVY

DURING THE AMERICAN REVOLUTION

1775 to 1778

MASTER MARINER, POLITICIAN,
BRIGADIER GENERAL, NAVAL
OFFICER AND PHILANTHROPIST

BY

EDWARD FIELD A. B.

PROVIDENCE
THE PRESTON & ROUNDS CO.
1898

TO MY FRIEND

HORATIO ROGERS, LL.D.

JUSTICE OF THE

SUPREME COURT OF RHODE ISLAND

INTRODUCTION

But slender justice has been rendered to the services of Esek Hopkins in the American Revolution. Historians could not omit all reference to the first Commander-in-Chief of the American Navy, but the manner in which some of them have mentioned him would seem to indicate that they wrote not from their fulness, but from their lack of knowledge concerning him. The only positive information most writers had of him, apparently, was that he had been dismissed from the naval service, and hence they inferred that he must have deserved his fate. The more satisfactory method of historical portrayal would have been to have narrated the causes that led to that treatment and let the reader draw his own conclusions as to the justice of it.

The narrow escape of various eminent characters in our national history from supersedure or condemnation, warns us that official action is by no means a sure guide to a just judgment. The machinations of a cabal of discontented generals at one time fomented trouble for Washington in the Continental Congress, while the jealousy of Halleck, when commanding our army in the late Civil War, well nigh accomplished the displacement of Grant.

Whatever my own estimate of Esek Hopkins may be, however, I have presented the facts just as I have gleaned them, that each may judge for himself what manner of man he was.

I have drawn my material entirely from official records, manuscripts and standard authorities. Of the very highest value have been the Hopkins Papers, preserved in the Rhode Island Historical Society, consisting of the official orders and letters of Hopkins while Commander-in-Chief, covering the whole period of his connection with the navy, and of a number of volumes of correspondence and other papers relating to other parts of his life.

The Hopkins Papers were deposited in the Rhode Island Historical Society, with the consent of the Hopkins heirs. It is remarkable that so many of them have been preserved after the years of neglect which they suffered, being stored in old attics and taken from place to place and exposed for sale. Some, doubtless, have disappeared, but those remaining comprise the greater part that relate to Hopkins' naval service.

These papers are preserved in four volumes the first being the letters and orders of the Commander-in-Chief. 1776–1777; the second consists of letters and miscellaneous papers 1728–1786; the third contains similar documents, 1776–1778; the fourth is a volume of type-written copies of various papers deposited in the national archives.

These copies were made some years ago at the suggestion of Richard S. Howland, Esq., editor of the Providence Journal, many inquiries having been made regarding the

official record of Hopkins service in the
navy. Mr. Howland requested that a search
be instituted at the several departments at
Washington for all the material relating to
Hopkins in possession of the national government, and that it be brought together for
historical purposes. In response to this
request, the departments very courteously
forwarded typewritten copies of all documents
bearing on the subject and they were entrusted to the Rhode Island Historical
Society for safe keeping.

Besides these papers, the writings of John
Adams contain much in regard to the proceedings in Congress when Hopkins was
under investigation by that body, while the
records of the State of Rhode Island testify
to his unremitting labors in the public service
for a long term of years. But it is no part
of my purpose to weary the reader by here
detailing all my authorities; suffice it to say
that those I have mentioned form the chief.

In preparing this volume the exact language of letters, orders, and official proceedings has been preserved as far as possible, as

it seemed to me to impart a clearer significance than when smoothed up or rounded out by a revising hand.

I desire to acknowledge my obligations to the Hon. Amos Perry, Librarian of the Rhode Island Historical Society, for his kindly courtesy in aiding me in procuring material, and to Mr. Fred A. Arnold, of Providence, who has permitted me to use his valuable collection of old prints in making many of the illustrations for this work.

EDWARD FIELD.

Providence, R. I., November, 1898.

CONTENTS

LIST OF ILLUSTRATIONS

ESEK HOPKINS

CHAPTER I

ANCESTRY AND EARLY LIFE.

EARLY in the affairs of Rhode Island, appears the name of Hopkins. Thomas Hopkins, the ancestor of many of those in New England who now bear the name, was one of thirty-eight men who joined in an agreement for a form of government for the little settlement which Roger Williams established at the head of Narragansett Bay, and to which he gave the name Providence.

It was an unpromising settlement at first, as all new ventures are apt to be, for it was the first free government to be established in the civilized world. Enemies without its borders scoffed at the idea of a government so unstable. Enemies within its borders, by intrigues with the neighboring authorities, sought to overthrow it, yet though tauntingly alluded to as a "nest of unclean birds" and said to be made up of those with minds too weak or too strong to assimilate with the other colonies, it grew and flourished, and from within its limits was quarried the foundation stone on which our national fabric rests—civil liberty.

With this infant community Thomas Hopkins identified himself, and ere the settlement had seen four years of existence, was already participating actively in its affairs. Called upon by his fellow townsmen to fill, many offices of public trust, he served successively as Commissioner, Deputy and Town Councilman. He was also for a time Town Sergeant; an ancient manuscript is yet preserved signed by Roger Williams, directing Sergeant Hopkins to warn certain townsmen to appear at the "Towne House" and give testimony in a case then pending, between Thomas Angell and Robert West. Thomas Hopkins was born in England, April 7, 1616, was the son of William and Joanna (Arnold) Hopkins, and, at his coming to Providence, was a young man twenty-four years of age.

The date of his marriage is not known, the name of his wife even is a subject of

conjecture, his great grandson,¹ who was sixteen years old at the time of his grandfather's
death, noted in his family record that she was
a daughter of William Arnold and a sister of
Governor Benedict Arnold. This has generally been admitted to be the case although
Austin in his *Genealogical Dictionary of
Rhode Island* makes no mention of it, but
another careful historical writer and genealo-
gist² has found that while there was nothing
to absolutely disprove this theory, there was
enough to create a doubt as to its accuracy.
Thomas Hopkins had three sons all of whom
married and had children. William Hopkins,
the eldest son, was a surveyor, a man of learning, and held numerous town offices. At the
time of King Philip's War when the Colonial authorities warned the people of the various towns to remove to Newport by reason
of its greater security from the depredations
of the savages, William Hopkins "stayed and
went not away," as the records quaintly note
this act of heroism. His father, however, on
the breaking out of the war, being well advanced in years, "with a part of his family

---

¹ Governor Stephen Hopkins.
² The late Albert Holbrook.

sought an asylum abroad to escape the perils incident to the struggle," and took up his residence at Littleworth, in the Township of Oyster Bay on Long Island, where he died in 1684.

In 1698 William Hopkins was commissioned "major for the main land," which gave to him the command of the military forces of the mainland settlements in the colony. He married Abigail Dexter, the widow of Stephen Dexter, who was a son of Reverend Gregory Dexter, pastor of the First Baptist Church in Providence, and by her had one child, a son named William. But few facts relating to him have been preserved: there is no record of the date of his birth, marriage or death, though his wife was Ruth Wilkinson, a daughter of Samuel and Plain (Wickenden) Wilkinson, her father being a son of Reverend William Wickenden, the successor of Reverend Gregory Dexter. William Hopkins junior was for a time in Providence, but he removed to what afterwards became the town of Scituate in Rhode Island, where he died some time between the eleventh of June and the ninth of October, 1738.

William and Ruth Hopkins had nine children, their names being William, Stephen,

Rufus, John, Hope, Esek, Samuel, Abigail and Susanna, two of their sons, Stephen and Esek, becoming conspicuous by reason of distinguished public service. Four of these sons, William, John, Samuel, and Esek followed the sea, and all but one were masters of vessels. William, the eldest son, "was remarkable for his dash and enterprise, his career being marked by many characteristics of a resolute and reckless nature." In evidence of this there is a well established family tradition that when a young man but nineteen years of age, being in London at the time of a riot which threatened the safety of the Royal Family "he promptly organized a force of sailors and loyal citizens, under the inspiring cry 'Fall in and protect the King', and rushing to the onset, quelled the disturbance, to the great gratification of the imperilled dignitaries." For this act of heroism he was the recipient of many royal favors. He was commissioned a colonel by King George I, but service in America being more to his liking he sold his commission and returned home. There is yet preserved among the possessions of the Rhode Island Historical Society a fragment of a coat which originally formed a part of a court suit presented to

William Hopkins for his gallantry on this
occasion. This suit was carefully kept by
him, and after his death the desire to secure
this interesting relic became so great among
his numerous descendants, that it was cut into
pieces, and the parts distributed among them.
The piece thus preserved came into the possession of the late Stephen Randall, who married one of the descendants, and by him was
presented to the society where it now remains.
Another brother, Captain John Hopkins, died
at sea, while yet another, Captain Samuel Hopkins, died at Hispaniola while on a voyage.
The services of Stephen Hopkins to the
colony of Rhode Island and to America are
a part of the nation's history. Esek Hopkins,
another son of William and Ruth Hopkins,
was born April 26, 1718, within the territory
now included in the town of Scituate. R. I.,
but then a part of the town of Providence.
The neighborhood about the Hopkins homestead farm was called by the Indian name of
Chopomisk, and was in the midst of a wild
and sparsely settled country. His boyhood
days were spent upon the farm, but upon his
father's death, being then "a stout, tall and
handsome young man," twenty years of
age, he journeyed to Providence, where he

obtained a berth on a vessel then about to sail
for Surinam, and entered upon a seafaring
life. Two of his brothers, John and Samuel,
were at this time masters of vessels which no
doubt influenced him in taking to the sea.

At this period the commercial activity of
Rhode Island was evidenced by ships from
her waters in all ports of the world. There
was hardly a vessel engaged in the carrying
trade in the colonies but what numbered
among its crew, or had for a master, a Rhode
Islander. Born and brought up within a colony with a navigable coast line of more than
two hundred miles, dotted here and there with
ships loading and unloading at the wharves,
or keels stretching out upon the sandy beach-
es, it was but natural that a spirit of adventure
should have been awakened among her people
for a life which offered so many opportunities
for advancement and gain, as well as affording
means for acquiring greater knowledge by
contact with the great world outside. "It
was no accident," says a learned writer, "that
from a period long preceding the War of the
Revolution, the term 'Rhode Islander' had
come to be synonymous with 'a born sailor.'"

Hopkins entered upon his new life with
all the spirit and zest which characterized the

seamen of those days. He soon rose to the command of a vessel and took a prominent rank among New England master mariners. When twenty-three years of age he married Desire Burroughs, a daughter of Ezekiel Burroughs, a leading merchant and ship master of Newport, R. I., the ceremony being performed in that town, by the Reverend Nicholas Eyres, on November 28, 1741. At this time he was living in Providence, but upon his marriage he took up his residence at Newport, from which port he sailed in command of various ships engaged in the carrying trade. About the year 1748, Hopkins removed from Newport to Providence, and at a general town meeting held on August 30 of that year, was propounded as a freeman of the town of Providence. It does not appear however, that he took the oath of fidelity required of all freemen until January 14, 1750, nearly two years later. During these years he was doubtless at sea, which precluded his appearing in open town meeting and swearing allegiance, as was the custom.

He early became interested in the cause of education, and almost the first official duty which he performed for the town was on a committee to have the care of the "townes

schole and of appointing a schole master."
Associated with him on the committee were
Nicholas Cooke, who afterwards became Governor of the colony, Joseph Olney, Elisha
Brown, and John Mawney, and all leading
men in the town affairs. The deep interest
which the committee gave to the duty of hiring
the school master, and the earnestness with
which they regarded the matter of education,
is shown in one of the articles of the indenture
executed by the committee and George Taylor, who was selected to direct the young
ideas in this town school for the year 1753,
for it was provided "he school or teach one
poor child such as said committee shall recommend gratis or for nothing during said
term." How much credit is due Hopkins
in this movement for the establishment of a
town school cannot of course be determined.
It is certain however, that up to this time there
had been no official action taken towards the
education of the youth of the town. William
Turpin many years before had served as
schoolmaster under some town sanction and
had carried on his instructions at his tavern,
but so far as any evidence is found, this was
the first school committee appointed to establish a place for instructing the children, and

from this small beginning developed the splendid system for which this town subsequently became widely noted.

Long years after this Hopkins was called to give his services in the cause of education, and for twenty years he was a trustee of Rhode Island College, now Brown University, and was highly esteemed by Manning, its distinguished president.

During what is generally termed the "Old French War," from 1754 to 1763, privateering was largely engaged in by the people of New England; Rhode Island merchants especially, fitted out at great expense numerous vessels to prey upon the commerce of the enemy; so enthusiastic were the privateersmen at this period and so intent were they upon the capture of desirable prizes, that not only ships hailing from ports of France and her colonies but those hailing from other countries were attacked, captured and taken into New England. Spain especially suffered from these captures, until at last formal complaint was made, through Mons'r d'Abreu, envoy extraordinary from His Catholic Majesty, to the King, and Rhode Island was promptly rebuked for these outrages or depredations, as they were plainly called, by

William Pitt, the Home Secretary, in his letter to the Governor of Rhode Island.

It is during this period that most of the references to Hopkins' early maritime adventures are found, and these are nearly all connected with the year 1757. That he commanded a privateer and was eminently successful in his cruises seems certain. Moses Brown of Providence, afterwards a leading merchant, wrote on February 23, 1757. "Capt. Esek Hopkins has Taken and sent in here a snow of about 150 tons, Laden with wine, oil, Dry goods &c to ye amount of about £6000 ye greater part of which will be Exposed to publick Vendue ye Tuesday next."

On the fifteenth of September John Brown of Providence, a brother of Moses Brown, and later his business partner, writing from Philadelphia says, "by a man from New Providence have heard that Capt Esek Hopkins & Ch. Waterman put in there about the middle of Aug Last to Cleane there Vessel & that they both saled on there Cruse about the 20th of Augst but had Taken nothing before, but what have heard of." Among the private papers left by Hopkins is an "acct sales of Sundry prize goods sold at Vendue taken by Capt Esek Hopkins and condemned in the

Court of Vice Admiralty of Connecticut." It
is dated at New London, November, 1757, and
certainly indicates that the days succeeding
the 20th of August were not spent unprofit-
ably. From these it would seem that he
was identified with vessels belonging to the
Browns. It was during the year previous to
these privateering ventures that Hopkins
established himself on a farm consisting with
subsequent purchases of more than two hundred acres, situated in the northern part of
the town. He had doubtless accumulated
a substantial store of this world's goods from
his voyages and from mercantile pursuits, for
he is called in deeds both mariner and shop
keeper, and was thus able to establish a com-
fortable home for his family which at the time
of this purchase, June 26, 1756, consisted of
his wife and six children, the youngest a
daughter not yet two months old.

He did not however remain ashore to pur-
sue the life of a farmer; the dash and excitement incident to life on board a privateer,
the enticing visions of greater profit from
successful voyages to the Spanish main and
the Indies proved more attractive than the
less exciting occupation of a country gentleman and farmer. His house, while he was

ashore, was a popular gathering place for his
large circle of acquaintances and friends and
he delighted in entertaining them; there were
hunting trips in the wild woods, shooting at
marks and other sports to occupy the time
on such occasions, but with all these pleasures
he found time to devote much attention to
carrying on his farm, employing many negroes
in this work. If he had slaves the fact has
not been handed down. There is an old indenture, dated in the year 1764, yet preserved,
that testifies to his taking one Edward Abby, a
free negro, one of the poor of the town, to
learn the art of husbandry. He doubtless
found the duties of farm life irksome and unin-
teresting, compared with the life at sea. During this time ashore his services had been
at the disposal of his fellow men, and he filled
many positions of honor and trust, being school
committee-man, fire ward, tax assessor, and, in
1762, with Moses Brown, John Smith, Benoni
Pearce, Nicholas Tillinghast and Benjamin
Man, served as director of a lottery authorized by the General Assembly, to raise £6000
for paving the streets of Providence.

In the field of political strife Hopkins took
a firm stand. He was uncompromising and
positive. In the election for colony officers,

in the spring of 1763. Elisha Brown, "a man
of great ability and enterprise," and a prominent politician, was a candidate for the office
of Deputy Governor. John Gardner, of Newport, being the opposing candidate. Hopkins
entered into the campaign with activity and
acrimony. It was in the days of what has
been known as the Ward-Hopkins controversy, when Samuel Ward and Stephen Hopkins, the two great leaders in the political life
of the colony, were arrayed against one
another, each advocating political opinions
and principles which kept the freemen of the
colony in a ferment of party strife. So evenly
were the forces of these two great leaders
matched that the elections were always close,
Hopkins being the successful candidate at one
time to be succeeded by Ward the next. During the period from 1758 to 1768 Stephen
Hopkins held the office of Governor from
March 14, 1758, to May, 1762; from May, 1763,
to May, 1765; and from May, 1767, to May,
1768; while Samuel Ward held the office during the intermediate years. It was in the
midst of this ten years struggle that Esek
Hopkins became a prominent figure. Elisha
Brown was on the ticket with Ward and the
fight was bitter. In addition to this, Hopkins

had a personal interest in the campaign : he
was one of the candidates for representative
to the general assembly from the town of Providence. The relations between Esek Hopkins
and his brother Stephen were always most
affectionate and friendly, and with the ties
of brotherhood he naturally became a strong
supporter of the Hopkins' ticket. Besides this
the relations between Mr. Brown and himself
were strained, the former having published
certain offensive information " in a Boston
Paper." In the midst of the contest Hopkins
prepared and caused to be published, in the
columns of the Providence *Gazette*, the following open letter:

" PROVIDENCE, April 16, 1763.

The public cannot but remember that
about two Years since Elisha Brown, Esq :
advertised in a Boston Paper, that Mr. Hopkins had two Sons at the Island of Hispaniola,
Masters of Flags of Truce. Now this very
identical Mr. Brown, who is at this Time a
Candidate for Deputy Governor of the Colony, has in this great Scarcity of Provision,
when one Half of the Country is almost ready
to starve for Want of bread, sent one of
his Sons in his large noted Brig called the

Wainscot, with about Six Hundred Barrels of Flour, and other Provisions on board, directly to Port-Louis, on the Island of Hispaniola, one of the most bare-faced Things that has ever been done in the King's Dominions; but what cannot a Man of Mr. Brown's Stamp do?

I would likewise observe, that this very Mr. Brown, in his Piece which he published before the Town Meetings[1] in the year 1760, entitled, Reflections upon the present State of affairs in this Colony; boasted, "That he had not since the first Commencement of the War, transported a single barrel of Provision, nor so much as a Firkin of Butter contrary to law"; and avers, among several other Things of the like Nature, that "the Exportation of such large Quantities of Provision, is one principal Cause of the great Scarcity of bread in the Colony." I would refer the Public to that whole Piece, and they will soon perceive the Views he had in altering the Administration, by comparing his present Conduct with the Pretentions he there makes

ESEK HOPKINS.

N. B. The Brig *Wainscot*, sailed from thence about the Month of September last."

---

[1] No mention of this is found among the Town Meeting records.

It no doubt had its effect and contributed to the defeat of the Ward ticket, for the spring campaign of 1763 resulted in the election of Stephen Hopkins of Providence, Governor, and John Gardner of Newport, Deputy Governor.

In his relations with his fellow men Hopkins was frank and outspoken, he made no attempt to conceal his opinion on subjects which aroused his interest or appealed to his sympathies, aggressiveness seems to have been a prominent trait of his character; it led him into controversies early in his political life, and it grew and increased in magnitude as his years advanced.

He was quick to penetrate trickery or deceit and quicker still to expose it, there was a strong individuality to his make up which sometimes operated more to his own discomfort and disadvantage than to right the supposed grievance or to elevate himself in the estimation of his fellow men. With a character strong and positive, coupled with the dictatorial manner of the master mariner of the times, he naturally made enemies and became easily drawn into controversies.

Not long after he had entered into political life this controversial tendency asserted itself;

2

perhaps in these days he would be called a
reformer, for, notwithstanding the bitterness
of his attacks on persons and measures, his
shafts were aimed at wrongs against his fellow
men although it must be said that insinuations
against those near and dear to him, as the
charges brought by Mr. Brown against his
sons, sometimes prompted him to defend if
not to revenge himself.   In 1753 Hopkins
was a member of a committee appointed by
the town to arrange for opening a town school.
This committee selected George Taylor for
the position of instructor, and he entered upon
his duties.   Taylor, besides gaining support
in this venture from the town and his pupils,
received also a salary of £10 a year from the
"Society for the Propagation of the Gospel
in Foreign Parts," he being the "Society's
schoolmaster;" for more than forty years he
acted not only as instructor, but as spiritual
advisor, to the younger element in the town.
On October 18, 1737, Mr. Taylor wrote to
this Society "that he teaches twenty-three
whites and two black children and catechises
them on Wednesdays and Saturdays, explains
to them the principles of religion which they
have learned by heart," and the Society in
its report for that year adds " this with Mr

Taylors' good life and conversation, comes
attested by Dr. McSparran." In 1776, nearly
forty years later, the Society's report says,
" Mr. Taylor, the Society's schoolmaster, notwithstanding his advanced age, gives constant attention to his school." With the
Reverend John Checkley, Reverend Doctor
McSparran and the Reverend James Honey-
man, all ministers of the Church of England,
Taylor was on the most intimate terms,
while his daughter, married the Reverend
John Graves, some time "Vicar of Chaplin,
in Yorkshire, in the Diocese of Chester,
a most pious and worthy clergyman," and
brother to the Reverend Matthew Graves,
missionary at New London, Conn. Taylor
seems to have carried on the school satisfac-
torily and, in addition to his duties as pedagog,
he filled the positions of justice of the peace,
member of the town council, and for several
years was president of that body. He acted
also as scrivener for the townspeople, and
many ancient documents, now preserved,
testify to his excellence as a penman. In
1762 Hopkins became involved with Taylor
in a bitter quarrel. It is difficult to ascertain
how it came about or the direct cause; it was
started however, by Hopkins in an open letter

signed by him and circulated about the town, there being no newspaper printed in Providence at that date to serve as a medium between the two disputants. Only one of the letters in this controversy has come to light. and as it furnishes all the information known regarding the trouble, it is here repeated in full from the original, on file with the Hopkins papers, in the possession of the Rhode Island Historical Society.

" To the Public.

A Brief Reply to a Paper signed by George Taylor, Esq., dated April 11, set forth as an Answer to one of mine. dated April 2.

I Observe a great Deal of Scurrility thrown out against me, and several Gentlemen in this Town; but all the answer I shall return Mr. Taylor, in respect to myself, and of my not writing my Piece, which he insinuates, is this, That whoever exposes the evil Practices of a Miser, may expect to receive ill Treatment: And as for the Gentlemen he hints at in his Piece, no Doubt they are able to Answer for themselves.—But this much I must suppose. that Mr. Taylor has taken a Suit for a Mortgage, in the Room of a Bond, and that seems evident from the Number of

Papers in the Case he has produced, which
are Fifteen, and in a Case for a Bank Bond
there should be but Three, Mr. Taylor says,
he drew but Thirty-two or Thirty-three of
the Bills of Cost, and Mr. Jackson the Rest,
as attorney to the Treasurer; but had Mr.
Jackson any Thing to do with them as an
Officer? for the Clerk examined, and the
Judge taxed them, no Doubt more than what
the Law allowed, in order to Colour their
own. Now let us see what Mr. Taylor says,
in Answer to my Charge against him, which
was, that he as an Officer took more than
double the Fees the Law allowed. Why
truly he says, some other People had done
wrong before him? And I answer, that every
Man that has behaved ill might say the same,
that there has been bad Men before them.
Mr. Taylor seems to confess that he had
done wrong, by being new in the Business; but
all that are acquainted with him, know that
he has held more Justice's Courts within
Twenty Years, than all the other Justices in
the County.—I would advise, that whenever
a Miser is put into an Office, that in the
Room of his being sworn to observe the Laws
of the Government he should be sworn to
follow his own Interest. Upon the Whole, I

think it is high Time there was a Stop put
to the exorbitant Fees not only of the
Judges but the Sheriffs also, who now exact
as much as will satisfy their avaricious Ap-
petites, without any Regard to the Laws
they are sworn to observe.

                              ESEK HOPKINS.
PROVIDENCE, April 18, 1762:"

Both these men emerged from this conflict
without apparent injury to their character or
standing in the community.   Taylor lived
for several years, enjoying the highest confidence of his neighbors, and was honored by
being elected to offices of especial honor and
trust.   He died in 1778, and by his will, executed on the eighth day of October of that
year, he made his son-in-law, the Reverend
John Graves, one of his executors.   Graves
"was the successor of the Reverend John
Checkley, of St. John's Church, in Providence,
and attended the service until July, 1776.
He then declined to officiate, unless he could
be permitted to read the usual and ordinary
prayers for the King, which he considered
himself bound by his ordination vows to offer
for him.   The patriotism of his hearers forbade this, and the consequence was that the

church was closed most of the time during the war of the Revolution."

The next year, as the time for the election approached, the two parties again prepared for the struggle. There was the same intensity of feeling, the same bitterness of political strife. Stephen Hopkins and Samuel Ward were the candidates for Governor, and the Ward-Hopkins controversy the issue.

Esek Hopkins was again a candidate for the legislature and active in the campaign. He was backed by strong and substantial men, the Brown Brothers, Nicholas, Moses and John. leading men of the town, men too whose influence was a power in the community. Hopkins had commanded their vessels, they knew his worth, they had had opportunities for a study of his character and capabilities, they believed in him and that confidence was reciprocated. With the Brown Brothers and with Joseph Brown he openly made political warfare against the secretary of the colony, Henry Ward, of Newport. He was tainted with Ward heresies and must be removed, his influence was powerful, and the freemen of the colony were warned to cast their ballots for a candidate more suitable to the Hopkins faction, and Hopkins, with the Browns, sent broadcast this circular:

"PROVIDENCE, April 2, 1764.

As the present Secretary will not be satisfied to enjoy his Office peaceably, but is constantly endeavoring, by every Means in his Power, to remove the Governor, Deputy-Governor and assistants, with whom he serves, from their Offices, it hath been thought just to set up some other Person for Secretary, who might be careful to do his Duty, and behave peaceably in his Office. And as Mr. William Richardson, a person every Way well qualified, is now Candidate for that Office, we ask it as a Favor of every Freeman to give him a vote.

> ESEK HOPKINS,
> NICHOLAS BROWN,
> JOSEPH BROWN,
> JOHN BROWN,
> MOSES BROWN."

The Brown and Hopkins candidate for secretary was defeated, Governor Hopkins however was elected, as was also Esek Hopkins. Henry Ward was too firmly entrenched in his position to be affected by the influences which made and unmade other colony officials, and he served in his office with honor and distinction for thirty-seven years, when death closed his long and useful public life.

The Browns and Hopkins had been staunch allies in this campaign, but a time was coming when the relation between these men would be strained, when all the power and influence which Hopkins possessed would be exerted against them, not on account of private motives or personal grievances, but because he believed it a duty he owed to the cause which he espoused. His action at this time shows his high patriotic character as no other act in his whole life ; it discloses an honesty of purpose, a determination to serve his country first, all else being subservient to this.

The following year Esek Hopkins was again elected to the general assembly, members of the lower house being then designated as deputies, and he the fourth deputy from the town of Providence. He did not however serve the full term for which he had been elected, in the service of the colony. The attractions of the sea were more to his liking, and the profits of successful voyages more alluring than the honors and excitement of political life, and on the " last tuesday in

August 1764," the day on which the Providence town meeting was in session, he came before the freemen there assembled, and stated " that he was bound in a few days out of the King's Dominions, to abide for a Long time, and that he could not represent the town any longer". His resignation was thereupon accepted, and the freemen proceeded at once to elect as his successor John Cole, Esq.. the moderator of the meeting. Before Hopkins entered again into political life great events had taken place, and greater ones were in store.

In February, 1765, Captain Owen, who had arrived in Providence on the 13th of that month from the West Indies, reported that "on the 30th ult., in Lat. 33 Long. 68, he spoke with Captain Campbell, in the Brig 'Gambia' of, and for New York, from the coast of Africa, who acquainted him of the safe arrival of Captain Esek Hopkins, of this Port on the Coast."

For nearly four years he continued at sea, making long voyages to Africa, China and the West Indies ; occasionally during this period he is reported by vessels entering New England ports, and his own safe arrival in Rhode Island is duly chronicled in the newspapers.

Upon returning to his native shores after his life at sea, Hopkins found that during his absence the town of North Providence had been incorporated, and his homestead fell within the lines of the new town. It was not long before the people of North Providence sought his services and advice, and at the spring election of 1768 he was selected as second deputy from the new town. Before this term for which he had been elected expired, he was again on the ocean; the Providence *Gazette* for March 16, 1769, reports in its marine intelligence, "Capt. Esek Hopkins from Surinam on the 16th ult in Lat 30, Long 62½ spoke the Brig 'Rose,' from Madeira for Philadelphia, out for 34 days, all well."

On the third of November following Captain Aulger, who had arrived in Providence that day from Surinam after a voyage of thirty-seven days, reported that he left at that place when he sailed Captains Esek, George and John Hopkins, all of Providence.

It was about this time, and quite likely while on this voyage that the only life portrait of Hopkins now extant was painted. This picture in which his figure appears represents a scene in a public house at

Surinam. It so happened that a large number of vessels hailing from Rhode Island
were at this time in port, and the masters
and supercargoes, taking advantage of this,
made arrangements for an evening's pleasure
ashore, to which a few other choice friends
were invited. It is the work of an English
artist by the name of Greenwood[1], who
was of the party, and who is said to have
been a noted portrait painter of that day.
All the figures are likenesses of the persons
who actually participated in the carousal,
and were esteemed very good likenesses
at the time. "Indeed" wrote the owner,
Dr. Edward Wild, many years ago, "the
resemblance of several of them can be clearly
traced in the features of their descendants
of the present day." The artist represents
himself as just passing out the door and
vomiting. Mr. Jonas Wanton, of Newport,
fat, round faced, asleep, and just being bap-
tised; Captain Ambrose Page, vomiting
into the pocket of Wanton; Captain Nicholas
Cook, afterwards Governor of Rhode Island,
under a broad hat, with a long pipe, seated
at table talking with Captain Esek Hopkins,

---

[1] Probably John Greenwood, an engraver and painter

SCENE IN A PUBLIC HOUSE IN SURINAM.

From the original painting by Greenwood, in the possession of Edward J. Cushing, Esq., North Providence.

wearing a cocked hat and left hand suspi-
ciously holding a wine glass. Mr. Godfrey
Malbone, of Newport, dancing, the shorter one
receiving the lesson, while Captain Nicholas
Power is acting as instructor; a Dutchman
seated on a chest nursing his leg, doubtless
having received a kick from one of the roys-
terers, and several others whose features are
not now identified. Several of the party, some
six or eight, were members of the Jenckes
family, through which family the picture
has descended to its present owner, Edward
J. Cushing, Esq., of North Providence. The
picture came into the possession of Mrs. Mary
J. Wild, whose mother was a Jenckes, soon
after her marriage, in 1819. It was then taken
from North Providence to Brookline, and
in 1825, as it had become somewhat defaced,
was turned over to a man by the name of
Laughton, a carriage and sign painter, of
Brookline, to be repaired. His touches were
of the crudest character, and before varnish-
ing it he took the liberty of repainting the
floor a dull yellow, thereby obliterating the
date and spoiling the perspective. It was
returned to North Providence to the old
mansion, the home of Mr. Cushing, in 1858,
where it now rests, and where it has been

nearly all of the time since 1800. It has received some injury since that time, yet it is still in good preservation. It is painted on bed ticking and is seventy-three and three-quarters inches long by thirty-six and one-half inches wide.

Besides being interesting as containing this portrait of Hopkins, it has some additional interest from containing a portrait of Hopkins' life-long friend, Captain Ambrose Page,[1] even though he may be represented in a rather undignified position.

The year 1771 again found Hopkins the choice of his townsmen for the legislature, and for the next three years he was returned as the first deputy from North Providence.

At this time he seems to have abandoned the sea, which he had followed for nearly thirty-five years. He had acquired a competence, and he doubtless felt that he could well afford to settle down on his farm and enjoy the companionship of his wife and family, from whom he had been separated much. He had earned a well merited reputation as a master mariner of great success,

---

[1] Capt. Ambrose Page married Sarah (Jenckes) Hopkins, the widow of Capt. Christopher Hopkins, who was the son of William, brother of Esek.

skill and ability, and his name was a familiar
one in all the ports of the maritime world.

During these years momentous questions
were agitating the minds of the American
Colonists.

It was a critical period in the affairs of
America, " the third and final period of the
constitutional revolution, the period which separated the colonies from the mother country." Already overt acts of violence against
British authority had taken place in Rhode
Island. July 19, 1769, the revenue sloop
" *Liberty* " had been seized by a party of Newport citizens and destroyed. In Massachusetts, the Boston riots had taken place, and
these conflicts between the populace and the
military authority showed plainly enough the
temper of the colonists, and that " oppression
drove wise men mad." North Carolinians
had nursed their grievances until patience
had become exhausted, and, on the 16th of
May, 1771, a large number of the people,
under the leadership of able and distinguished
men, became involved in conflict with the
governor at the head of a military force, re-
sulting in the death of twenty of the citizens
and nine of the soldiers of the King's army.
Following this, the people of Boston had

answered John Rowes' significant query, as to
how tea and salt water would mix, by a prac-
tical illustration in the waters of the harbor,
while the proceedings of the house of Bur-
gesses, of Virginia, had been the subject of
argument and action by Hopkins himself, in
connection with his associates in the legislature of the colony of Rhode Island.

And all these acts were like the low mut-
terings of the distant thunder, a warning of
a coming storm.

During this period, too, had occurred that
daring attack made by certain of the townsmen of Providence, on the British armed
sloop "*Gaspee*." This exploit was instigated
and carried out by a leading merchant and
a party of master mariners, aided by a
number of daring young men. The outrages that had been committed by the
"*Gaspee*," commanded by Lieutenant Duddingston, had borne particularly hard upon
the vessels sailing in Narragansett Bay, as
he had "made it his practice to stop and
board all vessels entering or leaving the
ports of Rhode Island, or leaving Newport
for Providence." So incensed had the people
of Providence become at this high handed
and unwarranted action of the British officer,

that the most heroic measures were taken
to rid the bay of this pestiferous craft, and
on the night of June 9, 1772, eight large
whale boats, containing upwards of forty bold
and resolute men, rowed quietly down the
bay to Namquit Point, just below the present
village of Pawtuxet, where the "*Gaspee*" had
grounded during the day. The vessel was
boarded and set on fire, and before daylight
the next morning burned to the water's edge.
During this attack Lieutenant Duddingston
was wounded. The audacity of the under-
taking was widely commented upon at the
time, and every effort was made by the British authorities to apprehend those connected
with it, but, notwithstanding the large number of persons involved, the secret was carefully kept, and to this day but few of the
names of those who took part in that summer
night's work are known. In later years, when
all danger had passed, the names of a few
became public. The leaders in this expedition were personal friends of Hopkins,
he had commanded vessels in which John
Brown, the instigator of it, was interested,
and Brown had taken great interest in
Hopkins' doings for many years. Abraham
Whipple, who commanded the party, was a

3

near relative[1]; he had sailed in the same ship
with Hopkins on many privateering ventures,
and there was between the two a warm friendship, while Hopkins' own son, John B. Hopkins, at the time a young man thirty years
of age, took a prominent part in the affair.
This expedition was hurriedly conceived and
carried out, there was no time to send mes-
sengers to distant parts to secure recruits,
and Hopkins, at his quiet home far away
from the sound of the drum, which summoned
the party together, heard nothing of this
water side proposition, but it is quite certain
that the doings of that night, and the names
of those participating, were well known to
him ere the last spark of the smouldering
hull of the *Gaspee* had ceased to burn.

The year 1774 was a year of preparation,
and the proceedings of the legislative bodies
in the colonies were significant of deep purposes. There was great interest exhibited
in the military force. This alone might have
caused a suspicion that there was a rebellious
spirit in the minds of the people if no other
signs were apparent, but there was no lack of

Abraham Whipple married Sarah Hopkins daughter of John
and Catherine Hopkins, Aug. 2, 1761.

such signs. Resistance to British authority
and oppression was on the lips of every man.
Night after night the taverns were thronged
with men with determined looks on their
faces, treasonable sentiments were the subject of their discourse. Men were associating
themselves together and obtaining charters
for independent military companies. Inflam-
ing articles were being printed on circulars
or in the columns of the colonial press, and
scattered throughout the land. ".A recipe
for making gunpowder was included among
the useful information in the household al-
manack." The colonies of America were the
abiding place of a restless, indignant and
excited people. Rebellion was rampant.
The year closed and his Britannic Majesty's
good subjects in America united in the time
honored supplication, "God save the King."

CHAPTER II

BEFORE the winter's snows had entirely disappeared from behind stone walls and other sheltered spots, the storm burst that had been brewing so long. In the grey of early morning, on April 19, 1775, the yeoman soldiery of Massachusetts and the King's troops met in a bloody encounter in the highways of Concord and Lexington. Actual warfare had commenced. Three days later the General Assembly of Rhode Island met at Providence; it was the last session previous to the May session, when the new government took its seat for the ensuing year.

There is no stronger way of showing the temper of the people at this moment than by the proceedings of this session. Every measure considered was for the defence of the colony. Committees were appointed to procure lead, bullets and flints; the charters of two of the independent military companies

were amended and the two organizations
consolidated. A committee previously appointed to proportion the powder, lead and
flints among the several towns made its
report. The eleventh day of May was set
apart as a day of prayer, fasting and humilia-
tion. A committee was appointed to wait
on the General Assembly of Connecticut " to
consult with them upon measures for the
common defence of the Five New England
Colonies." A committee was appointed to
take the care of the cannon, powder and other
warlike stores in the magazine, at Providence.
An army of fifteen hundred men was ordered
raised " to repel any insult or violence that
may be offered to the inhabitants and also,
if it be necessary for the safety and preservation of any of the Colonies, to march out of
the Colony, and join and cooperate with the
forces of the neighboring Colonies."

The passage of this resolution was not
without opposition. Joseph Wanton and
Darius Sessions, Governor and Deputy Governor respectively, opposed it, as did also
Thomas Wickes and William Potter, two of
the Assistants. The grounds of their opposition, as stated in the protest which they subsequently filed, being " that such a measure

will be attended with the most fatal consequences to our Charter priviledges; involve
the country in all the horrors of a civil war;
and as we conceive is an open violation of
the oath of allegiance which we have severally
taken, upon our admission into the respective
offices we now hold in the Colony." At the
spring election Wanton had been reelected
Governor; he refused to issue commissions
to the officers appointed to command the
troops to be raised; to attend the General
Assembly or take the oath of office, and even
neglected to issue the proclamation for the
observation of the day of fasting and prayer
designated by the legislature.

His position at this critical period was at
once discovered, and measures were taken
to deprive him of all his powers. Every
authority was forbidden to administer to
him the oath of office, and, that the business
of the colony might not be hampered, the
Secretary, Henry Ward, was authorized to
sign all commissions to officers, both civil
and military; the Deputy Governor was
clothed with certain powers, and the affairs
of Rhode Island went on under the leadership of Nicholas Cooke, who had been elected Deputy Governor.

The excitement caused by this action of
the Governor was soon followed by more
important and alarming events; the business of the government however was soon
straightened out, and the officers elected to
command the army of observation, as this
military body heretofore ordered to be raised
was called, received their commissions, duly
signed by Henry Ward, in time to assume
their positions and participate in the fight
of Bunker Hill. The result of this engagement filled the people of Rhode Island with
alarm, but its effect throughout the colonies
was encouraging and significant, and Franklin wrote, "Americans will fight, England
has lost her Colonies forever."

The alarm felt in Rhode Island was not
that of fear for the success of the cause, but
a fear that from her exposed situation, and
the proximity of the enemy, she would be
surrounded and made helpless before any
effort could be made at resistance. British
ships of war were cruising about in Narragansett bay, a formidable army was only a day's
march to the northward. It was time for immediate action for defence. Already the first
naval engagement of the revolution had
taken place. On the fifteenth of June one

of the sloops belonging to the colony, commanded by Captain Abraham Whipple, had attacked a tender of the British frigate *Rose*, chased her ashore on Conanicut Island and captured her.

On the 28th of June, 1775, the General Assembly met in Providence, to which place all the records and treasure of the colony had been removed some time before, from Newport, then the seat of the colony offices.

A signal station was ordered established at Tower Hill, a commanding eminence in the southern part of the colony, and Job Watson appointed signal officer, to give intelligence if any " squadrons of ships should be seen off." Beacons were also ordered set up in various parts of the colony, to alarm the country in the case of the approach of an enemy. On the 20th of July the people awoke to a stern realization of the situation of affairs. James Wallace, commanding the British fleet in Rhode Island, assembled his ships in line of battle before the town of Newport, and threatened to fire upon it unless the authorities complied with his request for provisions for his men.

At Providence this news was the subject

of great concern, and, on the 31st of
July, the Providence town meeting was
convened, and Deputy Governor Cooke elected moderator. Steps were at once taken
to defend the town, and fortifications were
ordered erected on a high hill, called Fox
Hill, commanding the harbor. The con-
struction of this work was placed under the
control of Captain Nicholas Power, and he
was ordered to consult and advise with Captain Esek Hopkins, Ambrose Page, Captain
John Updike, Samuel Nightingale, Jr., Captain William Earle, and Captain Simon
Smith, who were appointed a committee to
regulate the conduct of the battery to be
established at this point. Most of these
men were sea captains who had sailed on
privateers, and were doubtless selected on
account of their experience in the handling
of heavy guns on ship board. Esek Hopkins thus entered upon a quasi military
career remarkable as it was brief. The
knowledge of the handling of great guns
was limited almost entirely to that obtained
on ship board; there was but one fort in the
colony at this time, located on Goat Island,
in Newport harbor. This committee prepared a set of rules or regulations for the

conduct of this fort, which, in itself, is a
strong defence of the charge that they were
military men. It was nearly a month after
their appointment before they evolved these
regulations and submitted them for the ap-
proval of the town, before putting them into
effect; such were the crude methods in the
early days of the Revolution.

" Regulations of the Fox Point Battery,
Drawn by committee. Presented to the
Town in Town Meeting August 29 1775,

Voted one capt E Hopkins be appointed
to commd the Battery at Fox Hill.

Voted one luft that Samuel Warner

Voted one gunner Christopher Sheldon

" do 7 men to each gun Including officers that such be select'd from the town
Inhabits. as are acq'd with the use of Cannon and doe not belong to Any of the In-
dependt. Companys who Attending this
Duty be excused from the Militia Duties.

Voted that the Battery compy Appt a
capt & gunner for Each Gun out of their
compy.

Voted that upon any person quiting the
Battery compy the officers thereunto Belonging have power to sellect others as above
said to keep their number complete.

Voted that two Persons be app'd to Guard said Battery on Day who shall attend there on morning to Relieve the Night watch and Tarry until the Evening watch is Sett.

Voted that the Great Guns be No & Each persons name who belong to said Guns be Wrote on a Card & stuck on the Gun they may belong to that they may know where to repair in case of an Alarm

Vot'd that the Capt. Lieut & Gunner of said Battery have the Care of preparing & keeping the Stores Belonging Thereto in Good Order.

Voted that the Battery Compy Exercise their cannon once a month or oftener to Perfect themselves in the use of Great Guns.

it is recommended that 2 more 18 pounders be mounted at the Battery at Fox Hill.

> WILLIAM EARLE
> SIMON SMITH
> JOHN UPDIKE   *Committee.*
> ESEK HOPKINS
> AMBROSE PAGE
> SAML. NIGHTINGALE JR."

In order to facilitate the conduct of public business during the time when the

General Assembly was not in session, a committee had been appointed, called the Recess Committee, to act during the interim with full power in the premises. The situation at Newport, and indeed throughout the southern portion of the colony, demanded that a competent officer backed by a military force be located there, to protect the people from the outrages being carried on. This committee, therefore, selected Esek Hopkins for the position, and he was duly commissioned Commander-in-Chief, with the rank of Brigadier-General.

The commission issued to Hopkins and to William West, his able lieutenant, is yet preserved. It is signed by Nicholas Cooke, Deputy Governor, countersigned by Henry Ward, Secretary, and dated October 4, 1775. He was not appointed to this position by his brother, formerly the Governor, as has been stated.[1] His peculiar fitness for the responsibilities involved was the only consideration. The position needed a man of judgment and fidelity, and such a man was Esek Hopkins.

The position to which Hopkins was thus assigned was one requiring the greatest tact

---

[1] Spears History of our Navy, Vol. I.

and the exercise of a wise discretion. The
British commander, Wallace, backed by a
formidable fleet, well manned, and well
armed, was lying before the town. He was
in a position to distress the inhabitants with
little or no activity, and to destroy the town
itself with comparative ease.

He demanded provisions for his fleet,
which the town had been prohibited by the
colonial authorities from furnishing. Newport was in a desperate situation.

To this condition General Hopkins first
addressed himself; with a force of about six
hundred men he established quarters in the
town of Middletown, adjoining Newport,
and immediately undertook to straighten out
the troublesome affair. Upon the refusal of
the town authorities of Newport to furnish
the supplies demanded, Wallace had closed
the port. All ferry boats, market boats,
fish and wood boats, were prevented from
coming to the town. Provisions, wood and
other supplies were thus cut off, and the
town was "exposed to all those dreadful
consequences which must inevitably arise
through the want of the common necessaries
of life." So desperate had the position
become that the town council of Newport,

after seriously considering the whole matter,
prepared a memorial to the General Assembly, in which they prayed for some relief.
The safety of the town demanded that some
concessions be made, and upon the promise
that Wallace would raise the blockade,
negotiations were permitted, and General
Hopkins was directed to regulate the supplying of the ships with provisions. Additional instructions were also forwarded to
him at this time, and there is a firmness and
determination in these directions more significant than would first appear, for it was
ordered that he, "from time to time, remove the troops under his command from
place to place as he should think may best
tend to the general safety, and the peace
and happiness of the town of Newport; pay-
ing the greatest attention to, and having the
tenderest concern for, the true and lasting
peace, support, and relief thereof, still having
an eye and just preference to the general
safety, and the common cause of America."

A consultation was held between the town
authorities and the British commander, and
a plan discussed for some concessions. Both
sides faced the situation squarely, and Wallace declared a truce, under the conditions

specified in the following letter, sent to the town council of Newport:

" I will suspend hostilities against the town till I have further orders, upon their supplying the King's ships with fresh beef, &c. Let it remain neuter. The ferry and market boats to supply it unmolested. If the rebels enter the town, and break the neutrality, I hold myself disengaged, and at liberty to do my utmost for the King's service.

JAMES WALLACE.

His Majesty's ship, *Rose*."

There is no date to this letter, it was published, however, in the Providence *Gazette*, on December 9, 1775, in connection with other correspondence regarding the troubles at Newport; it was written however previous to November 15, for it is referred to in a letter of Hopkins' of that date. Thus, nearly eight months before the Declaration of Independence, the condition of war between England and the forces of the colony of Rhode Island had been recognized by James Wallace, commander of the British fleet in Rhode Island. He admits hostilities and rebellion, declares the people of Rhode

Island rebels, arranges under a truce a neutrality, and accords belligerent rights to the "rebels." Such a condition did not exist between the two opposing forces around Boston, but on the fifteenth day of November, 1775, Esek Hopkins, commanding a mere handful of soldiers, of the Rhode Island militia, was arrayed against Great Britain in open warfare.

By the terms of this truce, General Hopkins was prohibited from entering the town with his troops. Newport was to supply the fleet with provisions; in consideration of which the sources of her supplies were to remain unmolested. In the arrangements for the carrying out of the town's part of the neutrality, Hopkins had the entire management and direction. He appointed Samuel Dyer, Esq., of Newport, to superintend the delivery of the provisions.

In conducting these negotiations Hopkins showed himself to be possessed of sagacity, quiet firmness and discretion; in character very different from the irascible, irresponsible man, whom his enemies later represented him as being.

Without coming to an actual conflict of arms (which might have proved disastrous

to the Rhode Island forces), he did succeed
in bringing about a condition of affairs in
which the British commander tacitly recognized him as the duly commissioned commander of an army raised by the legislature
of the colony of Rhode Island, as constitutional a body as the Parliament of Great
Britian, and one recognized for over a century by British authorities as such, by sub-
mitting to the orders and directions of Samuel Dyer, Hopkins' duly authorized agent.

The contentions between Wallace and
the town authorities of Newport, regarding
supplies for the ministerial fleet, were pro-
longed through the entire time that Hopkins was in command of this station. The
correspondence passing between Hopkins
and the town of Newport discloses a determination on the part of the General to
conciliate the differences, yet to manage
the affairs firmly, avoiding if possible ex-
treme measures. From his " Headquarters,
Nov 15 1775 " he writes to the town of
Newport.

"GENTLEMEN

I received a copy of a letter,
signed by James Wallace, Commander of
his Majesty's ship *Rose*, together with your

4

approbations of the contents; In answer to which I am to let you know, that I will permit you to supply the ministerial navy now in your harbor, with fresh provisions, &c. provided the quantity be ascertained, and is no more than is sufficient, or has been heretofore made use of, and that under the inspection of a man that I shall appoint and authorize, and not otherwise, provided that he, said Wallace, with all the vessels and boats under his command and direction, let all the wood, market, and ferry boats pass &, repass together with their passengers and effects unmolested and unexamined, on failure or breach of which I shall immediately stop the supplies. This is all that can be expected in supplying the ministerial navy, except they remove out of cannon shot of the town of Newport.

I am, gentlemen, your humble servant

ESEK HOPKINS, Brigadier General."

These conditions the town desired modified, and the next day sent to him the following:

"NEWPORT, Nov 16, 1775.

SIR

Your proposal for settling a truce between the town of Newport and Capt.

Wallace we have received and examined, and as the word unexamined in your proposal seemes to us will not be complied with by Capt. Wallace, request you will leave the same out, as we apprehend it contrary to his instructions and the acts of Parliament, and are fearful it will greatly impede the wished for truce. I am, in behalf of the Town Council of Newport, Sir, your very humble servant,

WILLIAM CODDINGTON Council Clerk. To Esek Hopkins, Esq., Brigadier General of the forces in this Colony."

To this proposition Hopkins reluctantly consented in the following brief reply:

" HEAD QUARTERS Nov. 16, 1775 To the Worshipful Town Council of the town of Newport.

GENTLEMEN

I received yours this day, wherein your request the word unexamined may be left out of my proposal, which I now give you leave to do; but think it would be more for your interest to let it remain.

I am, gentlemen, your humble servant Esek Hopkins Brigadier General."

Negotiations were finally concluded and a more peaceful result attained than had been anticipated. In view of the threatening aspect, many of the inhabitants of Newport left the Island, taking all their property with them, and, it is said, " For four days the streets were almost blocked with carts and carriages of every sort seeking a place of safety."

From that day Newport, as a commercial center, began to wane. Previous to the Revolution the trade of Newport was greater than that of New York. During the three months ending the 10th of October, 1769, 3,000 hogsheads of molasses were entered at the Custom House, to say nothing of the quantity that was " run in," as smuggling was sometimes delicately called.

It is doubtful if Wallace ever intended to fire upon the town. It was of too much importance as a rendezvous and military station to be destroyed, and, indeed, for more than three years was occupied by the British as such. In addition to the powers conferred upon Hopkins as commander of the military force, he was specially directed, in the commission issued to him, to apprehend George Rome, a merchant of Newport,

he having "greatly assisted the Enemy and
proved himself entirely inimical to the Liberties of America." No part of the colony
sheltered more of the Tories and Royalists
than Newport. Many of the most wealthy
and influential men in the town were included among them; of these George Rome
was the most prominent and bitter against
the independent movement in the colonies.

George Rome, "a gentleman of estate
from Old England," was a wealthy merchant
of Newport, where he resided winters. He
was the owner of a fine estate in North
Kingstown, R. I., with an elegant mansion-
house which he occupied during the summer. This residence he called Batchelors
Hall, "my little country villa." The house
and the grounds around it were the most
elaborate of any in the colony. Here,
surrounded by a large circle of friends, he
entertained in a sumptuous manner. Invi-
tations to partake of his hospitality indicate
somewhat the nature of the entertainment
provided, for, writing to one of his friends,
he says: "My compliments to Colonel
Stewart; may I ask the favor of you both
to come and eat a Christmas dinner with
me at Batchelors Hall, and celebrate the

festivities of the season with me in Narragansett woods? A covey of partridges or
bevy of quails will be entertainment for the
Colonel and me, while the pike and pearch
pond amuse you." In the Stamp Act excitement he upheld the crown, and much
bitterness was aroused against him. In
1773, Dr. Franklin, while in London, obtained a letter of Rome's which he transmitted to this country. A copy of it was
forwarded to Rhode Island, and Rome was
called to account for the scandalous asper-
sion contained in it.

This letter was devoted to a general abuse
of the government, in which he attacked the
legislature, the courts and juries of the
colony, advised that the charter be annulled
and a government more dependent on the
crown be created. He asserted that "the
colonies have originally been wrong found-
ed. They ought to have been regal governments, and every executive officer approved
by the King. Until that is affected, and
they are properly regulated they will never
be beneficial to themselves nor good subjects of Great Britain." This letter was
written from his Narragansett home, on
December 22, 1767. When this attitude

of Rome's became known it produced much
excitement in the colony. Resolutions con-
demning his actions were passed in open
town meeting in several of the towns, and
at the October session of the General
Assembly, in 1774, he was brought before
that body on a warrant to answer for his
aspersions on the government. His answers, when questioned, were insulting and
evasive, and he was adjudged in contempt
and ordered committed to the common jail
in South Kingstown until the close of the
session. Here he remained for some time,
and upon his release, in fear of bodily harm,
for the most intense feeling had been aroused
against him, he fled on board the British
frigate " *Rose*," then lying in the bay. His
estates were confiscated, together with those
of others of his stripe. The order for his
apprehension, given to Hopkins, was subsequent to this, and it is supposed that he
afterwards returned to Newport and continued his seditious practices What eventu-
ally became of him is not stated.

But Hopkins did not disregard others in
Newport who were inimical to the cause of
liberty. He acted on the spirit of his commission if not by direct order, and took

possession, in behalf of the colony, of the
estates of Benjamin Brenton, the heirs of
Andrew Oliver, deceased, Jahleel Brenton,
and Thomas Hutchinson, as well as the
estate of Rome, and reported his action to
the Governor. These estates were declared
confiscated and placed under the control of
persons appointed by the General Assembly
to manage, and the action of Hopkins approved by that body; it even went farther
and declared that all deeds executed since
the fifth of October, 1775, by certain other
persons of Tory proclivities, be null and
void. A year later the property thus confiscated, belonging to George Rome, was
sold at public vendue to the highest bidder,
and thus, says Updike, "the great estates of
Mr. Rome were lost to his family forever."

The duties devolving upon Hopkins while
in command of this military post were varied
and perplexing, requiring the exercise of
great judgment and a wise discretion.

The situation of affairs was most delicate,
and any misstep would have brought about
a conflict between the King's forces, under
Wallace, and the colony troops. During
his command on Rhode Island a sloop, with
her cargo, arrived in the Seaconnet river on

the east side of the island of Rhode Island,
in charge of Captain Isaac Eslick, of Bristol,
R. I., and by him was turned over to the
care of Hopkins. The arrival of this vessel
disclosed a spirit of adventure and daring
which characterized the ship masters of the
times.

Captain Eslick, in command of a small
trading sloop, had been captured at sea by
one of the English war vessels cruising off
the coast. A prize master and crew had
been put aboard and ordered to take her
into Boston, while Eslick had been detained
aboard the British sloop of war," *Viper*." Not
long after this the British sloop sighted and
overhauled the sloop "*Polly*," belonging to
New York, commanded by Captain Samuel
Barnes, and bound thence for Antigua. A
midshipman, as prize master, and several
hands, were put on board, with orders to
proceed with the vessel to Boston. Eslick
was also transferred to the sloop to act as
pilot, encouraged with the promise that if he
successfully and faithfully piloted her into
Boston harbor he should be rewarded with
having his own boat with her cargo restored
to him. Eslick soon established friendly
relations with two of the original crew of the

sloop, and together they determined to out-
wit the prize master and carry the sloop into
Rhode Island. It was a most daring project,
and one having little promise of success.
Wallace's ships were cruising about the
lower part of Narragansett Bay, and even
extending their cruises, on occasions, into
Long Island Sound, so that the chances of
successfully running this blockade were well-
nigh impossible. Nevertheless, Eslick laid
his course, and with the assistance of his
two accomplices the vessel was successfully
brought into the Seaconnet river and turned
over to Hopkins. By this exploit Eslick
lost all chance of redeeming his own property, which was still in the hands of the
enemy, but at the risk of his life and the
sacrifice of his own vessel and cargo he had
saved valuable property belonging to others.
The circumstances of his action were communicated to the colony authorities, and
the General Assembly soon after ordered
two hundred and fifty dollars paid to Eslick
and fifty dollars each to his two associates in the business. The payment of this
amount was made a lien upon the sloop and
her cargo, and Hopkins was directed to hold
the vessel until these amounts were paid,

which was promptly done, the owners, doubt
less, being well pleased to escape so easily
from what otherwise would have been a
total loss. The troubles which had continued between the colony officers and the
duly elected executive, Governor Wanton,
were now brought to a close, the General
Assembly passing an act declaring the office
of governor vacant, and Hopkins, with
Captain Joseph Anthony and Mr. Paul
Mumford, were appointed a committee to
receive from the deposed governor the
charter and other state papers in his hands.
The duties devolving upon General Hopkins
were now becoming so arduous that he was
authorized to appoint a secretary; a com-
missary and a sutler were also ordered
attached to the brigade under his command.
Early in October, Wallace, having harrassed
Newport and the farmers along the southern
bay side, moved his fleet northward to the
harbor of Bristol, where, on the 7th of October, 1775, he assumed a threatening attitude and proceeded to make the same
demands for provisions. In order to give
his demand a show of determination he fired
a few shots into the town, without doing
any damage save producing the greatest

excitement and fear among the inhabitants.
The town authorities wisely complied with
his demands and furnished him forty sheep,
and the fleet withdrew after landing a small
force and plundering neighboring farms.
All of the towns on the sea-coast were open
to such attacks, and, had Wallace desired,
he might have sailed even to Providence
and enforced similar demands. In view of
the unprotected situation of the colony
Hopkins was recalled to Providence, and,
with Joseph Brown, dispatched on a tour of
inspection to ascertain what places should
be fortified and in what manner. Colonel
William West was left in command of the
troops. The result of this committee's labor
was a series of fortifications extending along
the bay side at all exposed points, the military force of the colony was largely increased, and garrisons established composed
of the companies in the respective towns
where these works were located.¹ Cannon
were shipped to the Island, and a number of
18-pound guns in the fort already constructed at Providence were put on carriages
for field artillery.

See my " Revolutionary Defences in Rhode Island."

The naval force of the colony was augmented and all precautionary methods of defence provided that were deemed necessary. Thus matters went on until Hopkins received his appointment from Congress as Commander of the Continental Navy; his services as a military commander covering a period of two months and eighteen days. During this time his services had been entirely administrative, the troops under his command had never been brought into action, and, so far as there is any evidence, not a charge of powder had been burned. This hardly justifies the assertion, made by a recent historical writer, that in the appointment of Hopkins to the position of Commander-in-Chief of the Continental fleet Congress erred in appointing a soldier rather than a sailor. Surely a service of thirty years and more on the sea, most of the time as master of a vessel, would seem to entitle a man to a greater proficiency as a master mariner than three months' service would entitle him to be classed as a military commander.

Hopkins was a man of many capabilities; as a politician he seems to have been wise, active and aggressive; as a military commander firm. careful and discreet. In his subsequent career, when he entered upon broader fields of service than those afforded in his own native colony, he became the subject of criticism and abuse, but above it all his noble character, high integrity, and pure patriotism show out distinct and clear.

CHAPTER III

TO a maritime colony like Rhode Island,
the importance of having a naval con-
tingent was recognized at the beginning of
the trouble with the mother country. As
early as June, 1775, when the General Assembly had ordered an army of fifteen hundred men raised for the defence of the
colony, provision had also been made for
the fitting out of two suitable vessels "to
protect the trade" of the colony.

The largest of these vessels was manned
with a crew of eighty men exclusive of officers, and equipped with ten four-pounders
and fourteen swivel guns, and named the
"*Washington.*" The smaller vessel was
called the "*Katy*" and manned with a crew
of thirty men.

Abraham Whipple, who had seen service in
the old French War, the commander of the
"*Gaspee*" expedition, and who afterwards

held important commissions in the Continental Navy, was appointed commander of
the larger vessel, and commodore of the
little fleet which, besides these two vessels, consisted of two row galleys of fifteen
oars to a side, mounting each an eighteen-
pounder in the bow and carrying a number
of swivel guns. Each galley was fitted to
accommodate a crew of sixty men. Hardly
had this fleet been put in commission, in
fact before the row galleys had been fully
constructed, when the commodore's ship
and a tender to the frigate " *Rose*," of Wallace's fleet, met in conflict, and in the engagement which followed, Abraham Whipple
had the honor of discharging the first gun
upon the ocean, at any part of his Majesty's
Navy in the American Revolution.

Some time previous to the fourteenth of
June the British commander had captured
two packets belonging to some of the inhabitants of Providence; one of these Wallace
had fitted up as a tender, which was being
used to intercept the coasting trade and
annoy all craft sailing on the bay.

This being brought to the attention of
Deputy Governor Cooke, for the colony was
without a governor at this time, on account

of the Wanton episode, he dispatched a
spirited letter to Wallace on the 14th in
which he demanded the reasons for his action
in stopping vessels and generally annoying
the inhabitants. He also demanded the return of the packets thus seized. Wallace
was always brief and to the point in his
official correspondence, and on the fifteenth
he sent the following answer:

"His Majesty's Ship *Rose*
Rhode Island June 15 1775.

SIR: I have received your letter of the
14th inst although I am unacquainted with
you or what station you act in, suppose you
write in behalf of some body of people:
therefore previous to my giving an answer
I must desire to know *whether* or *not* you
or the people on whose behalf you write,
are not in open rebellion to your lawfull
sovereign and the acts of the British legislature

I am sir your most humble and obedient
servant

JAS. WALLACE

To NICHOLAS COOK ESQ."

Before the ink with which this letter was
written had fully dried, one of these very

5

packets that the Deputy Governor had
demanded restored, and which had been
fitted as a tender, was chased ashore on
Conanicut Island in Narragansett Bay and
destroyed. The details of this first engagement on the sea between Great Britain
and the colonies are obtained entirely from
British authority, and are thus described by
the commander of the tender, Master Sav-
age Gardner, in his log yet preserved in the
British archives. ".About 6 o'clock as our
tender was standing off and on between
Gold Island and the North Point of Conanicut Island they saw a sloop standing down
the river. Our tender hove too to speak
her. She hailed the tender and told them
to bring too directly or he would sink them
directly. Fired a shot which the tender
returned and kept a smart fire on both sides
for about half an hour when another sloop
joining and bringing our tender between
the fires that they had no opportunity of
getting off, tho' made two or three tacks
right off. By accident the Swivel cartrages
blowing up and the musquet cartridges near
expended. Thought most prudent to run the
Tender on shore to save the men which was
accomplished near the N. P. of Conanicut

Island. Only a petty officer and one man wounded by the powder blowing up. Tho' constant fire on them at their landing. Night coming on they being closely pursued separated and 'got safe on board the ship by noon next day.

Gunners stores lost in the sloop, viz. Bright musquets 11, Marines ditto 7. Cutlasses with scabbords 17, Bayonettes with scabbords 9, Marines ditto 7. Ships pistols 12, cartouch Boxes, with Belts and straps 12, Swivels 4. Aprons of lead 4, Swivel irons and saddle one each, Pikes 8. Cases of wood 2, Musquet cartridge box 2. Powderhorns 3, priming irons 6. Powder in Swivel cartridges 50 Pounds cartridges. 9 Pounders 2 do, ½ Pounders 40 Round Shot. Do 40 Grape 40, Musquetshot 15 pounds, Pistol Shot 9 Pound.

Boatswains Stores viz. Rope 2inch 30 fem., 12 inch 50 fem. Blocks of 2 inch double 2, larger of 8 inch 3, thimbles 12. Marline spikes 2. 1 Foremast steering sail and a mizr. F. J. G. Sail 1 Hatchett, 2 Logglines and 15 Hammocks.

Carpenters stores viz. 1 driveryard, 1 fore J. Mast steering Sailyard. 1 Tarperline.

Pursers stores viz. 1 Puncheon, 1 Barrel."

This exploit of Whipple's, together with the knowledge that he had been instrumental in the destruction of the "*Gaspee*," greatly exasperated Wallace, and he addressed him the following succinct and highly expressive letter:

"Sir: You Abraham Whipple, on the 10th June 1772 burned his Majestys vessel the *Gaspee* and I will hang you at the yard arm.

JAMES WALLACE."

To which Whipple briefly replied:

"Sir James Wallace Sir Always catch a man before you hang him

ABRAHAM WHIPPLE."

This little squadron was kept busily engaged in patrolling the waters of the bay, and at the time of the threatened attack on Newport was ordered to coöperate with the militia under Hopkins. While thus engaged a request was received from the Continental Congress to Governor Cooke that the Rhode Island fleet be dispatched to intercept two ships, which, it was learned, were bound to Canada with military stores, but the larger ship being then on a

voyage to Bermuda, and the situation in Rhode Island remaining unchanged, it was deemed unadvisable to send the smaller vessel on this expedition.

On Monday, the 21st day of August, 1775, the General Assembly of Rhode Island convened at Providence. At this session the first suggestion for the establishment of a Continental fleet was made, and from this suggestion the American Navy owes its origin. It was embodied in a resolution of instructions to the Rhode Island delegates to the Continental Congress, passed on August 26, for them to present to that body, that the sentiments of the colony might be plainly set before it. This resolution, with its preamble, cleared the way for another resolution passed on the following May, whereby Rhode Island severed all allegiance to Great Britain two months to a day before that remarkable declaration was made at Philadelphia. These instructions, prepared by the legislature of Rhode Island, were as follows:

"Whereas, notwithstanding the humble and dutiful petition of the last Congress to the King, and other wise pacific measures taken for obtaining a happy reconciliation

between Great Britain and the colonies; the
ministry, lost to every sentiment of justice,
liberty and humanity, continue to send
troops and ships of war into America, which
destroy our trade, plunder and burn our
towns, and murder the good people of these
colonies.—

It is therefore voted and resolved, that
this colony most ardently wish to see the
former friendship, harmony and intercourse,
between Britain and these colonies restored,
and a happy and lasting connection established between both countries, upon terms
of just and equal liberty; and will concur
with the other colonies in all proper measures
for obtaining those desirable blessings.

And as every principle, divine and human,
require us to obey that great and fundamental
law of nature, self-preservation, until peace
shall be restored upon constitutional principles; this colony will most heartily exert
the whole power of government, in conjunc-
tion with the other colonies, for carrying on
this just and necessary war, and bringing
the same to a happy issue.

And amongst other measures for obtaining this most desirable purpose, this Assembly is persuaded, that the building and

equipping an American fleet, as soon as possible, would greatly and essentially conduce to the preservation of the lives, liberty and property, of the good people of these colonies; and therefore instruct their delegates, to use their whole influence, at the ensuing Congress, for building, at the Continental expense, a fleet of sufficient force, for the protection of these colonies, and for employing them in such manner and places as will most effectually annoy our enemies, and contribute to the common defence of these colonies.

And they are also instructed to use all their influence for carrying on the war in the most vigorous manner, until peace, liberty and safety, be restored and secured to these colonies upon an equitable and permanent basis." [1]

On Tuesday, October third, these instructions were presented to the Continental Congress by one of the delegates from Rhode Island. No action was taken on that day relative to the suggestions contained therein, but it was referred to the following Friday for consideration and made

[1] Records of the Colony of Rhode Island, vol. 7, p. 367

the special order of the day. On that day,
however, it was again referred, finally coming
up for action the seventh day of October.
The suggestion of a measure of such exten-
siveness produced a spirited debate, participated in by Samuel Chase, of Maryland;
Eliphalet Dyer and Silas Deane, of Connecticut; Stephen Hopkins, of Rhode
Island; Robert Treat Paine, Samuel Adams
and John Adams, of Massachusetts; the
Rev. Dr. Zobly, of Georgia; Peyton Randolph, of Virginia; John Rutledge and
Christopher Gadsden, of South Carolina.
" It is the maddest idea in the world to
think of building an American fleet," said
Chase, " its latitude is wonderful we should
mortgage the whole continent," but he
added, I believe, " we should provide, two
swift sailing vessels."

Gadsden was inclined to be cautious
about accepting so broad a measure as the
" Rhode Island plan." He believed, however,
that it was absolutely necessary " that some
plan of defense, by sea, should be adopted."

John Rutledge wanted to know how
many ships were to be built and what they
would cost; until this was stated he could
not form an opinion; and, that the whole

subject might come before the Congress in
a comprehensive manner, he offered a resolution that a committee "be appointed to
prepare a plan and estimate of the American
fleet." This resolution was seconded by
the Rev. Dr. Zobly, of Georgia, who added:
"Rhode Island has taken the lead I move
that the delegates of Rhode Island prepare
a plan giving us their opinion:"

Samuel Adams suggested the difficulties
such a committee would be under without
knowing the wishes of Congress: "such a
committee can't make an estimate, until
they know how many ships are to be built,"
said he.

The debate then became general, and is
delicately alluded to by John Adams as
"lightly skirmishing." Gadsden charged
his associates with trying to throw the
whole subject into ridicule. He believed
that so important a suggestion should be
seriously considered "out of respect to the
colony of Rhode Island who desired it."
Deane resented the attempt to make light
of so important a subject: "let it be seriously
debated," said he, " I don't think it romantic
at all."

John Adams, in his memoranda of debates

in the Continental Congress, notes that: "The resolution to refer the matter to a committee was defeated." It appears, however, that it was subsequently so referred, for on the 13th of October, Congress, taking into consideration the report of the committee appointed to prepare a plan for a navy, after some debate, voted "that a swift sailing vessel to carry ten carriage guns and a proportionable number of swivels with eighty men be fitted with all possible dispatch for a cruise of three months and that the commander be instructed to cruise eastward for intercepting such transports as may be laden with warlike stores and other supplies for our enemies and for such other purposes as the Congress shall direct."

A committee was appointed to prepare an estimate of its cost and to contract for the fitting out of the same; it was also decided at this time that another vessel be fitted out for the same purpose, and that an estimate of the expense of this be submitted. Mr. Deane, Mr. Langdon and Mr. Gadsden, were appointed on the committee. On the 30th of October this committee submitted its report, and it was resolved "That the second vessel ordered to be

fitted out on the 13th inst be of such size
as to carry fourteen guns and a proportionable number of swivels and men." Two
other vessels were also ordered to be put
into service, one to carry not exceeding
twenty guns, and the other not exceeding
thirty-six guns, "for the protection and
defense of the United Colonies, as the Congress shall direct." A navy was now
assured; the Rhode Island plan had been
accepted. Stephen Hopkins, Joseph Hewes,
Richard Henry Lee and John Adams, were
added to the committee already appointed
to carry into effect the resolves of Congress
with all possible speed.

This committee, consisting of seven members, was known as the Naval Committee.
This committee immediately addressed itself
to the important duty referred to it.

John Adams afterwards wrote: "The
pleasantest part of the labors for the four
years I spent in Congress, from 1774 to
1778, was in the Committee on Naval
Affairs. Mr. Lee and Mr. Gadsden were
sensible men and very cheerful, but Governor Hopkins, of Rhode Island, above
seventy years of age, kept us all alive.
Upon business, his experience and judgment

were very useful. But when the business of the evening was over, he kept us in conversation till eleven and sometimes twelve o'clock. His custom was to drink nothing all day until eight in the evening, then his beverage was Jamaica spirits and water. It gave him wit, humor, anecdotes, science and learning. He had read Greek, Roman and British history, and was familiar with English poetry, particularly Pope, Thompson, and Milton, and the flow of his soul made all of his reading our own, and seemed to bring in recollection in all of us all we had ever read * * * Hopkins never drank to excess, but all he drank was immediately not only converted into wit, sense, knowledge and good humor, but inspired us all with similar qualities."

Stephen Hopkins and John Adams, representing two important maritime colonies, were the most active and influential members of this committee. They were firm friends then and they remained so ever afterwards.

Christopher Gadsden, another member of the committee, was a friend of Esek Hopkins, and was in constant correspondence with him. This committee at once undertook

the work of procuring and fitting out the
vessels ordered, and by the fifth of No
vember, 1775, had so far progressed in
the accomplishment of the duty devolving
upon it as to select Esek Hopkins, of
Rhode Island, as commander of the fleet,
and on that day he was officially notified
of his appointment. It was undoubtedly
the influence of Stephen Hopkins that
brought this about, seconded by the friendly
interest of John Adams and Christopher
Gadsden. It is not unreasonable to believe
that the reputation of Esek Hopkins, as a
successful and experienced master mariner,
was well known in Philadelphia at that
time among shipping merchants and ship
masters, and even with other members of
the Naval Committee he may have had
some acquaintance if not a closer friendship.
A Newbern, North Carolina, newspaper cor-
respondent, about this time, refers to Hopkins
as "a most experienced and venerable sea-
captain." On the day following his selection by the committee for this important
and honorable position, his brother sent to
him the following letter, expressing the hope
that he would accept the appointment.

"Philadelphia, Nov' 6, 1775.

Dear Sir:

You will perceive by a letter from the Committee, dated yesterday, that they have pitched upon you to take the Command of a Small Fleet, which they and I hope will be but the beginning of one much larger.

I suppose you may be more Servicable to your Country, in this very dangerous Crisis of its affairs by taking upon you this Command than you can in any other way. I should therefore hope that this will be a sufficient Inducement for you to accept of this offer. Your Pay and Perquisites will will be such as you will have no Reason to complain of. Such officers and Seamen as you may procure to come with you, may be informed, that they will enter into Pay from their first engaging in this service, and will be intituled to share as Prize one half of all armed Vessells, and the one third of all Transports that shall be taken.

You may assure all with whom you converse that the Congress increase in their Unanimity, and rise Stronger and Stronger in the Spirit of opposition to the Tyrannical Measures of Administration

I am your affectionate Brother

STEP HOPKINS.'

It was while Hopkins was in command of the military force stationed at Newport that he received the notice of his appointment to the command of the Continental fleet, but it was not until the latter part of December that he was relieved of this command. In the meantime the situation at Newport remaining one of grave uncertainty, Governor Cooke applied to General Washington for a regiment to coöperate with the Rhode Island troops in the defence of the island. He also asked that General Charles Lee be sent to take command of the post which Hopkins was about to vacate, and on the twenty-first of December, General Lee arrived in Providence and immediately assumed command of the forces around Newport. During the time intervening between Hopkins' departure and the arrival of General Lee, Colonel William West held the command of the post. On the twenty-second day of December, the day after

---

¹ Hopkins Mss. Rhode Island Historical Society.

General Lee assumed the command vacated by General Hopkins. Congress confirmed the appointment of Esek Hopkins as Commander-in-Chief of the fleet to be raised, and also appointed the following officers for the several vessels:

Dudley Saltonstall, Abraham Whipple, Nicholas Biddle, John Burroughs Hopkins,	Captains.
John Paul Jones, Rhodes Arnold, —— Stansbury, Hoysted Hacker, Jonathan Pitcher,	First lieutenants.
Benjamin Seabury, Joseph Olney, Elisha Warner, Thomas Weaver, —— McDougall,	Second lieutenants.
John Fanning, Ezekiel Burroughs, Daniel Vaughan,	Third lieutenants.

The rank given to Hopkins was intended to correspond in the navy to that held by General Washington in the army. The title bestowed upon him seems to have

varied: sometimes he was addressed as
commodore, sometimes as admiral, while
even in official communications from the
president of Congress and the Naval Committee he was given both these, as well as
the full title named in the resolution of
Congress appointing him.

Hopkins set out for Philadelphia in the
early part of January, in the sloop "*Katy*,"
afterwards called the "*Providence*," of the
Rhode Island navy. This vessel was commanded by captain Abraham Whipple, and
had also on board a number of seamen who
had been enlisted in Rhode Island to serve
in the fleet. After a voyage enlivened by
taking a small vessel and three prisoners, the
"*Katy*" arrived in Philadelphia, January 14.
Her arrival was duly communicated to Governor Cooke by Samuel Ward, a member of
Congress from Rhode Island, on January 16,
who said: "Our seamen arrived here day
before yesterday. Those concerned in the
naval department are highly pleased with
them. Their arrival gives fresh spirit to the
whole fleet."

When Hopkins arrived in Philadelphia
he found a scene of great activity. The
Naval Committee had promptly complied

6

with the directions of Congress, and the ships for the fleet, of which he was to take the command, were being assembled in the Delaware river.

Eight vessels of varying tonnage were selected from the available merchantmen, hurriedly altered over for the accommodation of larger crews than they had originally been designed for, and pierced for heavy guns. The ship selected as the flag-ship was formerly a merchantman named the "*Black Prince*." She had recently arrived from London under the command of John Barry. Maclay, in his History of the Navy, says: "She was a small vessel, but was considered a stout ship of her class, and was named the '*Alfred*,' after Alfred the Great who was commonly regarded as the founder of the British navy." She carried twenty-four guns, and Captain Dudley Saltonstall[1] was assigned to her command. The second was called the "*Columbus*," formerly the

merchantman "*Sally*," a thirty-six gun ship,
twelve and nine pounders on two decks, and
forty swivels, and carrying five hundred men,
and was to be commanded by Captain Abraham Whipple, the captain of the "*Katy*," which
had brought Hopkins from Providence to
Philadelphia. The third was a fourteen gun
brig called the "*Andrea Doria*," after "the
great Genoese admiral of that name," and was
commanded by Captain Nicholas Biddle.
The fourth was a fourteen gun brig named the
"*Cabot*," after Sebastian Cabot the discov-
erer, and was under the command of Captain John Burroughs Hopkins' a son of the
Commander-in-Chief.

The "*Katy*," of the Rhode Island navy,
upon her arrival in Philadelphia, was taken
into the continental service and named the
"*Providence*." "She was named," says John
Adams, "for the town where she was pur-
chased, the residence of Governor Hopkins
and his brother Esek, whom we appointed

his "age 44 years, Heighth 5 ft 9 in, Sandy Colored hair, light
complexion, light hazel eyes and thick set." Captain Saltonstall
was a brother-in-law of Silas Deane, son of Gen. Gurdon Saltonstall and grandson of Gurdon Saltonstall, Governor of Connecticut,
1708-1724.

' John Burroughs Hopkins left no descendants, and no portrait
of him is known to exist.

the first captain." This vessel was a brig
and carried twelve guns. The rest of the
fleet consisted of a ten gun sloop called
the "*Hornet.*" Captain William Stone, and
the "*Wasp*" and "*Fly.*" eight gun schooners.

The "*Wasp,*" "*Hornet*" and "*Fly.*" were
expected to be annoying pests to the enemy,
and hence their names.

On the fifth of January the Naval Committee had formulated their directions to the
commander of the new navy in the following :

"Orders and Directions for the Commander
    in Chief of the Fleet of the United
    Colonies.

You are to take care that proper discipline good order and peace be preserved
amongst all the ships, and their companies,
under your command.

You are to direct the several captains to
make out and deliver monthly or oftener
an exact return of the officers Seamen and
marines on board of each respective vessel
noting their particular condition and cir-
cumstance—also the quantity and quality
of provisions and stores of every kind
together with the state of the respective
ships—which returns or copies of them

you are to transmit to Congress or a Committee by them appointed, to receive such returns, as often as opportunity offers.

You are by every means in your power to keep up an exact correspondence with the Congress or Committee of Congress aforesaid, and with the commander in chief of the Continental forces in America.

As by your instructions you are impowered to equip such Vessels as may fall into your power, and to appoint officers for such Vessels—as often as this shall happen you are by the very first opportunity to transmit to Congress or the Committee aforesaid, the burthen, force and manner of equipment of such vessels, together with an exact list of such officers as you may appoint, in order that their appointment may be confirmed by Congress or others be appointed in their stead.

You will be particularly careful to give such orders and instructions, in writing, to the officers under your command as the good of the service may in every case require—to devise or adopt and give out to the Commanding officer of every ship, such signals, and other marks and directions as may be necessary for their direction.

You are to take very particular care that all the men under your command be properly fed and taken care of when they are in health, as well as when they are sick or wounded. You will also very carefully attend to all the just complaints which may be made by any of the people under your command and see that they are speedily and effectually redressed for on a careful attention to those important subjects the good of the service essentially depends.

You are always to be exceedingly careful that your arms, as well great as small, be kept in the very best condition for service and that all your cartridges, powder shott and every accoutrement whatsoever belonging to them be kept in the most exact order: always fit for immediate service.

You will carefully attend to such prisoners as may fall into your hands—see that they be well and humanely treated—you may also send your prisoners on shore in such convenient places where they may be delivered to the Conventions, Committees of Safety or inspection in order to their being taken care of and properly provided for.

You will also give proper orders and directions to the Captains or Commanders

of the Ships or Vessels under your command in case they should be separated by
stress of weather or any other accident in
what manner and at what places they
shall again join the Fleet.

> STEP. HOPKINS
> CHRIST. GADSDEN
> SILAS DEANE
> JOSEPH HEWES."

About the time that Hopkins arrived in
Philadelphia, Gadsden, of the Naval Committee, was suddenly called to South Carolina, which colony he then represented
in congress, to take command of his regiment, the first regiment of foot. On the
tenth of January he sent to Hopkins a letter,
detailing, at some length, the situation in
Charlestown, and advising him of the men
there to whom he could look for advice and
assistance. The statements in the letter
give unmistakable evidence that the Naval
Committee had contemplated that the fleet
should be used, in the proposed operations,
against the enemy at Charlestown. This
letter was as follows:

"PHILAD". 10ᵗʰ Janry 1776

Dᴿ. SIR

Inclosed is Copy of an Order from the Committee to Capᵗ. Stone sent by Directions of Congress on an Application from Maryland wᶜʰ. it is necessary you shou'd have—

I also take the Liberty to send you a List¹ of the Field Officers & Captains of two Regiments of Foot & three Companies of Artillery all Provincials Station'd in Charles Town Sᵒ. Carolina, shou'd you go there, upon your Arrival off the Bar

---

¹ Among the Hopkins Papers in the Rhode Island Historical Society, is this list of the officers referred to, as follows : Christ Gadsden Colonel of the First Regiment of foot in South Carolina; Lieutenant Colonel, Isaac Huger; Major, Charles C. Pinkney; Captains, William Cattel, Adam McDonald, Thomas Lynch Jr., William Scott, John Barnwell, Thomas Pinckney, Edmund Hyrne, Roger Saunders, Benjamin Cattel.

SECOND REGIMENT.

Colonel, William Moultrie; Lieutenant Colonel, Isaac Motte; Major, Alexander McIntosh; Captains, Francis Marion, Peter Horry, Daniel Horry, Nicholas Eveleigh, James McDonald, Isaac Harleston, William Mason, Francis Huger, Charles Motte.

OFFICERS OF ARTILLERY.

Lieutenant Colonel, Owen Roberts, Esq ; Major, Hon. Barnard Elliott; Captains, Barnard Beekman, Charles Drayton, Syms White.

the Pilot will informe you what Officer is
at Fort Johnson or any of the nearest
Batteries to you. from whom you may
depend on all the Assistance they can
give, they are most of them Gentlemen of
considerable Fortunes with us who have
enter'd into the service merely from Principle & to promote & give Credit to the
Cause, they take it by Turns to be at the
Fort, & the Zeal & Activity of all of them
are such that you can't happen amiss let
who will be there—

In Charles Town my particular Friends
Mʳ. Lowndes, Mʳ. Ferguson, Coll Powell,
Mʳ. Benjᵗ Elliott, Coll Pinckney. Mʳ. Drayton.
Mʳ. Timothy & the Revᵈ. Mʳ. Tennant a
Countryman of yours will introduce you to
many others, who will all be glad to have an
Opportunity of obliging you & promoting
the Service.

I wrote Yesterday to Mʳ. Ferguson one of
the Gentⁿ just mention'd by Way of Georgia.
by a Gentleman I can depend on who will
destroy my Letter should he be taken, in
this Letter I have hinted to look out for
you, & be ready to assist you at a moment's
Warning— The two large ships seen off
of Virginia the 29ᵗʰ of last Month we are

told were not bound there, however you will
know more certainly by the Time you get
out of the Capes I make no doubt—I hope
you will be able to effect that Service, but
whether you may or not, sooner or later I
flatter myself we shall have your Assistance
at Carolina, when you may depend on an
easy Conquest or at least be able to know
without Loss of Time when off our Bar the
Strength of the Enemy, & shou'd it be too
much for you prudently to encounter w^h I
hardly think probable if soon attempted w^t.
the assistance to be depended on from us
you may in such Cases retreat with great
Ease, Safety & Expedition—

Wishing you every Success you can possibly wish yourself—

I am D^r. Sir y^r. most hble Servt.

CHRIST GADSDEN

P. S.   Pray make my Compliments to
Capt Salterstall & the rest of your Captains,
& I shall be obliged to you if you go to
Carolina to introduce them to any or all the
Gentlemen I have mention'd who I am sure
will be glad to show them every Civility in
their Power—   I hope Capt. Whipple is
better—

One of the Maryland Gent'. M'. Alexander a Delegate of that Colony tells me there is a very good Ship of about 20 guns there easily fitted out w^h. he is in hopes will join you with the '*Hornet*' & '*Wasp*'. & that he shou'd press it to be done this I mention by the by,—

To Esek Hopkins Esq. Commander in Chief of the Fleet of the United Colonies."[1]

The letter to Capt. Stone of the "*Hornet*," alluded to in the correspondence, directed him to coöperate with Hopkins, and, for its importance in connection with the events which subsequently occured, is here presented:

"PHILADELPHIA 10th January 1776

SIR:

We are ordered by Congress to signify to you that you are with the '*Hornet*' & '*Wasp*' under your Command to take under your convoy such Vessels as are ready for the sea as shall be committed to your Care by the Com of Safety at Maryland & see them safe through the Capes of Virginia and without a moments loss of time after

[1] Hopkins Papers, Vol. II. p 3

this service is done you are to go to the
Capes of Delaware & proceed upwards till
you join the fleet, or in case of its having
sailed receive such orders as may be left for
you by Esek Hopkins Esq Commander in
Chief of the Fleet of the United Colonies

W^ch orders you are to Obey

> STEPHEN HOPKINS
> CHRIST GADSDEN
> SILAS DEANE
> JOSEPH HEWES

To William Stone Esq Commander of the
Sloop '*Hornet*' In the service of the
United Colonies."[1]

The day after Hopkins' arrival, Gadsden
addressed to him another letter; he was
about to depart from Philadelphia on a
pilot boat in response to his orders to join
his regiment. This letter gives additional
information as to the expected operations
of the fleet. It was as follows:

> " PHILADELPHIA 15 Jany 1776
>
> SIR
>
> I last night received my orders to go
to Carolina & expect to set out on Thursday

Hopkins Papers, Vol. II. p 33

morning from one of our Pilot Boats now at New Castle in which I shall take my chance—Should you come our way if you think proper to let me know to morrow or next day what signal you will show when off our Bar, you may depend on my keeping a good Look-out for you & to let no Body know the signal but where it is necessary

I am Yr most hble Sert

CHRIST GADSDEN "

In compliance with the request made by Gadsden, Hopkins devised a signal by which the arrival of the fleet might be known, and informed him that "Some one of the Fleet if together or the small sloop if a lone will highst a Striped flagg half up the flying stay." This paragraph in Hopkins' own handwriting is added to the original letter of Gadsden's, yet preserved.' It will thus be seen that it was the intention of the Naval Committee that the fleet, among other movements, should proceed to the Carolinas and coöperate with the land forces against the enemy at that point.

Hopkins Papers, Vol. II, p 4.

The special orders given Hopkins by the Marine Committee form an important part of the events which later occurred, and, as they must be considered in making a correct estimate of his conduct, they are here given:

" To ESEK HOPKINS, ESQUIRE,
Commander in Chief of the Fleet of the United Colonies.

SIR: The United Colonies directed by principles of just and necessary preservation against the oppressive and cruel system of the British Administration whose violent and hostile proceedings by sea and land against these unoffending colonies, have rendered it an indispensible duty to God, their country and posterity to prevent by all means in their power the ravage, desolation and ruin that is intended to be fixed on North America. As a part and a most important part of defence, the Continental Congress have judged it necessary to fit out several armed vessels which they have put under your command having the strongest reliance on your virtuous attachment to the great cause of America, and that by your valour, skill and diligence,

seconded by the officers and men under
your command our unnatural enemies may
meet with all possible distress on the sea.
For that purpose you are instructed with
the utmost diligence to proceed with the
said fleet to sea and if the winds and
weather will possibly admit of it to proceed directly for Chesapeak Bay in Virginia and when nearly arrived there you
will send forward a small swift sailing
vessel to gain intelligence of the enemies
situation and strength. If by such intelligence you find that they are not greatly
superior to your own you are immediately
to enter the said bay search out and attack,
take or destroy all the naval force of our
enemies that you may find there. If you
should be so fortunate as to execute this
business successfully in Virginia you are
then to proceed immediately to the southward and make yourself master of such
forces as the enemy may have both in
North and South Carolina in such manner
as you may think most prudent from the
intelligence you shall receive; either by
dividing your fleet or keeping it together.

Having compleated your business in the
Carolinas you are without delay to proceed

northward directly to Rhode Island, and attack,
take and destroy all the enemies naval force
that you may find there. You are also to seize
and make prize of all such transport ships
and other vessels as may be found carrying
supplies of any kind to or any way aiding or
assisting our enemies. You will dispose of all
the men you make prisoners in such manner
as you may judge most safe for North
America and least retard the service you
are upon. If you should take any ships or
other vessels that are fit to be armed and manned for the service of the United Colonies,
you will make use of every method for procuring them to be thus equipped. You will
also appoint proper officers for carrying this
matter into execution, and to command said
ships as soon as they can be made ready for
the sea. For this purpose you will apply to
the several assemblies, Conventions and
Committees of safety and desire them in
the name of the Congress to aid and assist
you by every way and means in their power
for the execution of this whole service.

Notwithstanding these particular orders,
which it is hoped you will be able to
execute, if bad winds or stormy weather,
or any other unforseen accident or disaster

disable you so to do, you are then to follow
such courses as your best judgment shall
suggest to you as most useful to the American cause and to distress the enemy by all
means in your power. January 5, 1776.

> STEPHEN HOPKINS
> CHRISTOPHER GADSDEN
> SILAS DEANE
> JOSEPH HEWES'"

There was another project, however, not
mentioned in the orders, that had been
discussed both by Congress and the Naval
Committee, which was of greater importance
to the colonies at this time than the operations around Charlestown and other points
on the southern seaboard, and will find its
place in the events that subsequently took
place.

It was the intention of the Naval Committee to have the fleet sail early in January,
but a severe spell of cold weather set in,
the Delaware was frozen over, and obstructed
the passage of the ships down the river. It
was about this time that the first flag ever
hoisted on an American war vessel was flung

---

¹ From the original on file in the State Department, Washington, D. C.

7

to the breeze, and occurred when Esek Hopkins, the commander of the squadron, was received on board the "*Alfred*," his flag-ship.

Ever since Hopkins' arrival in Philadelphia he had been busily at work with the Naval Committee, arranging the details for the conduct of the expedition. At last the day came when all these arrangements were completed, and Hopkins was ready to take command of the little squadron of the United colonies.

Lying at anchor, amid the floating ice, lay the eight vessels of the new navy, their forms distinctly outlined against the winter sky.

The morning was clear and cold. Shortly before nine o'clock a barge put off from the "*Alfred*" and was rowed to the slip at the foot of Walnut street, where, without any delay, Hopkins stepped aboard and the barge returned through the floating ice to the flagship. Crowds of people lined the wharves and shore lands, while the shipping in the harbor was appropriately decorated as befit the occasion.

As Hopkins gained the deck Captain Dudley Saltonstall gave a signal, and First Lieutenant John Paul Jones hoisted a yellow silk flag bearing "a lively representation

NICHOLAS BIDDLE.

.

of a rattlesnake " and the motto " Don't tread
on me."

As this standard fluttered in the cold crisp
air the crowds along the water front burst
into cheers, and the guns on the shipping
and the artillery ashore pealed out its salute
to the flag.

With this simple ceremony the navy of
the colonies went into commission, but it
was a ceremony of deeper significance to
Hopkins, for with this act he had the honor
of being the first who dared to unfurl the
American flag in defiance of a powerful foe.

This was an event, too, of such importance
that Gadsden, on the eighth day of February, presented to Congress, as a memorial of
the occasion, " an elegant standard such as
is to be used by the commander in chief of
the American Navy, being a yellow flag
with a lively representation of a rattlesnake
in the middle in the attitude of going to
strike and these words underneath ' Don't
tread on me.'" It is unfortunate that the
first flag of the navy should not have been
preserved ; it hung for some time near the
president's chair in the congress room, but
it subsequently disappeared without leaving
any trace behind.

The cold weather continued and the ice held the ships from sailing. Late in the month, on the 27th, Hopkins wrote to the Naval Committee:

" GENTLEMEN

The River holds still froze so much that the Pilots will not undertake to carry us from here   But perhaps we may sail before the thing's can come for the small sloop by Water think it will be best to send some of the most necessary things by land such as some of the swivel guns Some musket ball some old Canvas & six 20 feet oars."

On the tenth of February, 1776, the squadron was ready to sail, and had rendezvoused at Cape Henlopen.   All of the officers and men had not arrived on board the ships, and Hopkins sent from his flag-ship an imperative letter for them to " make what dispatch you can as the fleet will sail the first wind."

Hopkins now promulgated an elaborate code of signals, and issued the following orders to the captains of the vessels in his fleet:

" Orders given the several Captains in the fleet at Sailing from the Capes of Delaware Feby 1776.

SIR

You are hereby ordered to keep Company with me if possible, and truly observe the Signals given by the Ship I am in but in case you should be Separated in a gale of wind or otherwise, you then are to use all possible means to join the Fleet as soon as possible, but if you cannot in four days after you leave the Fleet, you are to make the best of your way to the Southern part of Abacco (one of the Bahama Islands) and there wait for the Fleet fourteen days— but if the fleet does not join you in that time, you are to cruise in such places as you think will most annoy the Enemy and you are to send into Port for Tryal, all British Vessels or property or other vessels with any supplies for the Ministerial Forces, who you may make yourself Master of to such places as you may think best within the United Colonies.

In case you are in very great danger of being taken you are to destroy these orders and your signals

ESEK HOPKINS

Commr in Chief"[1]

---

[1] Letters and orders of the Commander in chief, in Rhode Island Historical Society, page 5.

A few days later, however, the ships were manned and ready to sail, and on the seventeenth, the wind being favorable, the squadron got under weigh and sailed out on to the broad Atlantic, and before nightfall had disappeared below the horizon.

CHAPTER IV

WHILE it was the intention of the Naval Committee that the fleet should cruise to the southward and operate against the British ships stationed along the coast as far down as Georgia, there was another project in view which had been discussed by the committee as well as by Congress itself. It was a matter of so much importance that it had not been discussed outside of the secret sessions of Congress, and, in the Naval Committee, only behind closed doors. So well had the secret been kept that it is doubtful if it were known to any one in the fleet but Hopkins, and even to this day it has never been considered in any account of Hopkins' first cruise with his squadron. In the early days of the American Revolution the scarcity of powder was one of the most alarming conditions with which the authorities had to deal. The supply from England had been

entirely cut off, and British cruisers swept the
sea, interfering with its importation. Up to
this period in the history of the colonies powder mills had not become numerous, and those
already erected certainly were not of a capacity
to turn out a quantity and quality sufficient
to meet the demands of actual warfare.
At the very time preparations were being
made to equip the fleet and put it in commission, Washington wrote, " Our want of
powder is inconceivable, a daily waste and
no supply presents a gloomy prospect."
Already this want had been discussed by
Congress and a plan for supplying it formulated. Nearly a month before, on November
29, information was laid before a secret session of Congress held that day, that there
was "a large quantity of powder in the
island of Providence," and it was forthwith
"ordered that the foregoing committee [1]
take measures for securing and bringing
away the said powder: and that it be an
instruction to the said committee, in case
they can secure said powder to have it
brought into the port of Philadelphia or to
some other port as near Philadelphia as can

[1] Naval Committee.

Commodore Hopkins.

Commandeur en Chef van Amer. Flotte.

From the original in " Geschichte der Kriege," 1778.

Portrait Plate 2.

be with safety." [1] In the orders given Hopkins before sailing this object is not mentioned, but that it was part of his plan of
action is evident from the orders which
Hopkins issued to his captains upon sailing
from the Capes, wherein he directs them " to
make the best of your way to the southern
part of Abacco (one of the Bahama Islands)
and there wait for the fleet fourteen days."
It would seem, therefore, from this, that two
objects were in view when the fleet sailed :
first, to harrass the British ships along the
coasts of the southern and New England
colonies, and second, to proceed to the
island of New Providence and secure the
powder and such other stores as were contained in the forts located there. With
these directions Hopkins sailed.

At the very outset of the cruise the de-
pressing influence of sickness was felt
throughout the fleet. "we had many sick
and four of the vessels had a large number
sick with the small pox," wrote Hopkins,
some weeks later. Soon after starting the
wind came on " to blow hard " from the
north east. The prospects of weathering

[1] Secret Journals of Congress.

the capes in mid winter were no more promising a hundred years ago than they are to-day. Hatteras had its dangers then as now. Notwithstanding the heavy gales the fleet kept well together until the second day out, when the "*Hornet*" and "*Fly*"[1]

[1] "A list of Seamen and Landsmen that came out of the Capes of Delaware in the '*Fly*.'

Hoysted Hacker	Capt
John Fanning	Lieut
Robert Robinson	Master
William Weaver	Steward and Cooper
John Downey	Boatswain
Thomas Bayes	Seaman
Joseph Johnways	"
Joseph Shereman	Landsman
John Young	Midshipman
William Pierce	Seaman
John Yorke	"
Joseph Breed	Landsman
Christopher Crandale	"
John Cooke	"
Daniel Scranton	"
John Clarke	Cooper
Quaco Chadwick	Seaman
Weden Carpenter	Landsman
Stephen Fowler	"
Parker Hall	"
Samuel Tyler	"
Peleg Johnson	Seaman
Reuben Daye	Landsman
Machesan Chase	Landsman
Wm McWhoton	"
Lawrence Ash	Seaman
John Chadwick	Boy

disappeared from sight and the former did not again join the squadron.

When the condition of the fleet was brought to Hopkins' attention, he decided to make his course for the Bahamas into

Jno Lon Hacker	Boy
Lavin Dashield	Mate
Philip Jestes	Seaman

PRISONERS

James Huts	Wm Boann
James Powel	Frank Carey
Michael Trony	Dragon & Surinam Wanton negroes"

(From the original among the Hopkins Papers.)

The following list of officers on board the Fleet is found among the Hopkins Papers in the Rhode Island Historical Society, and, while it has no date, it doubtless gives the personnel of the ships at the time the fleet sailed.

"OFFICERS ON BOARD THE FLEET.

Officers on Board the 'Alfred'

Benj Seabury .	Lieutenant
Jonathan Pitcher	do
Jonathan Maltbie	do
John Earle .	Master
Thomas Vaughan	1st Mate
Philip Alexander	3d Mate
Walter Spooner	Midshipman
Robert Saunders	,,
Charles Buckley	
Rufus Jenckes	
George House	
Esek Hopkins Jr	,,
Francis Varrel	Boatswain
Joseph Harrison	Surgeon
James Thomas	Gunner

warmer latitudes; besides this he had
learned, previous to sailing, that on account of the severity of the weather the
enemy's ships had all sought refuge in the
harbors along the seaboard, and that he must

Officers on Board the 'A. Doria'

James Josiah	1st Lieutenant
Elijah Warner	2d ditto
John McDougall	3 ditto
Benjamin Dunn	Master
William Moran	1st Mate
John Dent	2d ditto
John Margeson	3d ditto
William Reynolds	Midshipman
William Lamb	..
Dennis Leary	..
Evan Bevan	..
Alex McKenzie	..
Wm Darby	..

Officers on Board the 'Cabot'

Elisha Hinman	1st Lieut
Thomas Weaver	2d Lieut
John Welch	Capt Marines
John Kerr	Lieut ..
John Sword	Midshipman
Ephraim Goldsmith	..
Abel Frisbie	..
Peter Richards	..
David Roberts	Gunner
Rich'd Potter	Boatswain
Richard Fordham	Carpenter

'Providence'

| William Grinnell | Lieutenant |
| John Rathbun | ditto |

be the aggressor and approach a dangerous
coast with little prospect of gaining any advantage. Much had been left to his discretion by his orders, and unforeseen accidents
and disasters had disabled him from the outset; he therefore signaled the ships, the
course was laid for the island of Abacco, and
the lookout off Charlestown bar watched in
vain for the "striped flagg half up the flying
stay." The island of Abacco is the northerly
of the Bahama group, and lies about thirteen
leagues to the northward of the island of

Wm Hopkins .	Master
Sam. Brownel	actg ditto
John Margeson	1st Mate
Joseph Brown	2d ditto
John McNeal .	3d "
Joseph Hardy	Midshipman

'*Columbus*'

Joseph Olney .	2d Lieut
Ezekiel Burroughs	3d "
Joshua Fanning	Master
Daniel Beears	Midshipman
Rogers	Mate "

In addition to the names of men serving on board the "*Alfred*"
Nathaniel Cooke, of Cumberland, R. I., and John Fiske, of
Northborough, Mass., enlisted as marines, in October, 1776.

Nathaniel Cooke was born in the town of Cumberland, April 13,
1745. In June, 1776, he was drafted, and served one month as a
private in a company of minute men commanded by Col. George
Peck, and later in the year served a further term of one month.
In October he enlisted on board the "*Alfred*," John Paul Jones

New Providence, the objective point of the
expedition. For many years this island had
been a favorite point of attack. Seventy
years and more before, it had been attacked
by the French and Spaniards, the fort blown
up, the church and other buildings burnt,
and the governor and many of the principal inhabitants carried away into captivity;
this was in July, 1703. Not satisfied wtih
this, however, the attacking party returned
again in October and completed the destruction of the place. So completely was
the island devastated that it is said "when
the last of the governors appointed by the

Commander, then lying at Holmes Hole, Buzzards Bay. Almost
immediately afterwards the vessel put to sea, cruising to the eastward. During this cruise she took seven prizes, one of which was
the British ship "*Mellish*," bound for Quebec, one of the richest
captures of the war ; for she had on board eleven thousand stand
of arms and the same number of suits of clothing destined for the
British army, and several brass field pieces. Cooke served on the
"*Alfred*" for a period of nine months, and in October, 1777,
returned to his old company commanded by Col. George Peck.
He took part in Spencer's expedition to the island of Rhode
Island, and in August, 1778, participated in Sullivan's expedition
and the battle of Rhode Island.

   He served in various parts of Rhode Island with the militia while
the British was in possession of Newport and was honorably discharged at the end of hostilities. He died in the town of his
birth, September 27, 1846. For this account of his service and
for the order for prize money I am indebted to Frank A. William-
son, Esq., the great great grandson of Nathaniel Cooke.

lords proprietors, in ignorance of the Spanish raid, arrived in New Prov-
idence, he found the island
without an inhabitant." An
excellent harbor, with deep
channels sufficient for vessels
drawing twelve feet of water,
made it a safe refuge in a
locality full of coral reefs and
numerous islands. Deserted
and abandoned as a well regulated community, it soon
became the resort of pirates,
and was a common rendez-
vous for these buccaneers
and ocean highwaymen, "the
notorious Blackbeard being
chief among the number."

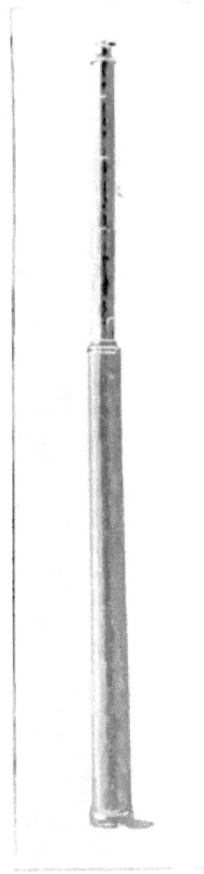

The depredations of these
villainous crews were reported
time after time to the merchants of London and Bristol, till at last, driven desper-
ate by their losses, they united in a petition
to the crown to again take possession of
the island and restore order. In compliance
with this petition, Captain Woodes Rogers
was deputized as the first crown governor,

and sailed for the island where he arrived
during the year 1718. Captain Rogers was
a man well fitted for the position; while he
cannot be classed as a pirate himself, he had
sailed for years as master of various privateers, and during the reign of Queen Anne
his exploits are calculated to suggest piracy
more than anything else. He was a man of
great force, and accustomed to rule with des-
potic sway. During one of his cruises he
rescued Alexander Selkirk, a Scotchman,
whom he found on the island of Juan Fer-
nandez, where he had lived alone for four
years and four months. Captain Rogers
speedily brought about a better condition
of affairs. Many good families settled on
the island, and it entered upon an era of prosperity. Nassau was the government seat, situated on the northern coast along the slope
of a gentle hill facing a land locked harbor,
and was protected by two forts, Fort Nassau
at the west, and Fort Montague at the east.
A dangerous bar lay off the entrance to the
harbor from the sea, while the two approaches
by the inside courses from the eastward and
the westward were amply protected by these
forts.

Hopkins was thoroughly familiar with the

neighborhood. Nearly twenty years before he had been reported at New Providence cleaning his vessel, and, undoubtedly, he had sailed in and out between the islands time and time again.

The fleet arrived at Abacco on the first of March, and on Saturday evening the second day of March, two hundred marines, under the command of Captain Samuel Nicholas, and fifty sailors, under the command of Lieutenant Thomas Weaver, of the "*Cabot*," who was well acquainted with the island, were embarked on some small vessels that had been captured. The men on board were ordered to keep below deck until the boats got in close to the island, it being Hopkins' intention that they should land instantly and take possession by an assault from the rear, before the inhabitants could be alarmed. This, however, was rendered abortive, as the forts fired an alarm on the approach of the fleet. The boats then ran in and anchored at a small key three leagues to windward of the town of Nassau, and from thence Hopkins dispatched the marines, with the sloop "*Providence*" and the schooner "*Wasp*" to cover their landing.

On Sunday morning, March 3, 1776, the

whole force landed at the east end of the island and moved upon the smaller fort, Fort Montague, situated halfway between the place of landing and the town of Nassau. Only a slight resistance was made by the force within the fort, five guns being fired at the attacking party, but without doing any damage. The garrison then withdrew to the larger fort, and the marines and sailors took possession of the abandoned work, where they remained and rested that night. That evening Hopkins received word that about two hundred men from the inhabitants of the town formed the only defence of the other fort, Fort Nassau. Desiring to accomplish his object without bloodshed or loss of life, Hopkins issued the following manifesto:

" To the Gentlemen Freeman and Inhabitants of the Island of New Providence

The Reasons of my landing an armed force on the Island is in Order to take possession of the Powder and Warlike stores belonging to the Crown and if I am not opposed in putting my design in Execution the Persons and Property of the Inhabitants shall be safe. Neither shall they be suffered to be hurt in Case they make no resistance

ISLAND or N
Showing th
FIRST AMERIC
Unde
COMMODO

HOG ISLAND

SAU

FORT
MONTAGUE
Captured Mar 1 1776

D E N C E

LANDING PLACE OF
AMERICAN FORCES
Sunday Morning
Mar 3 1776

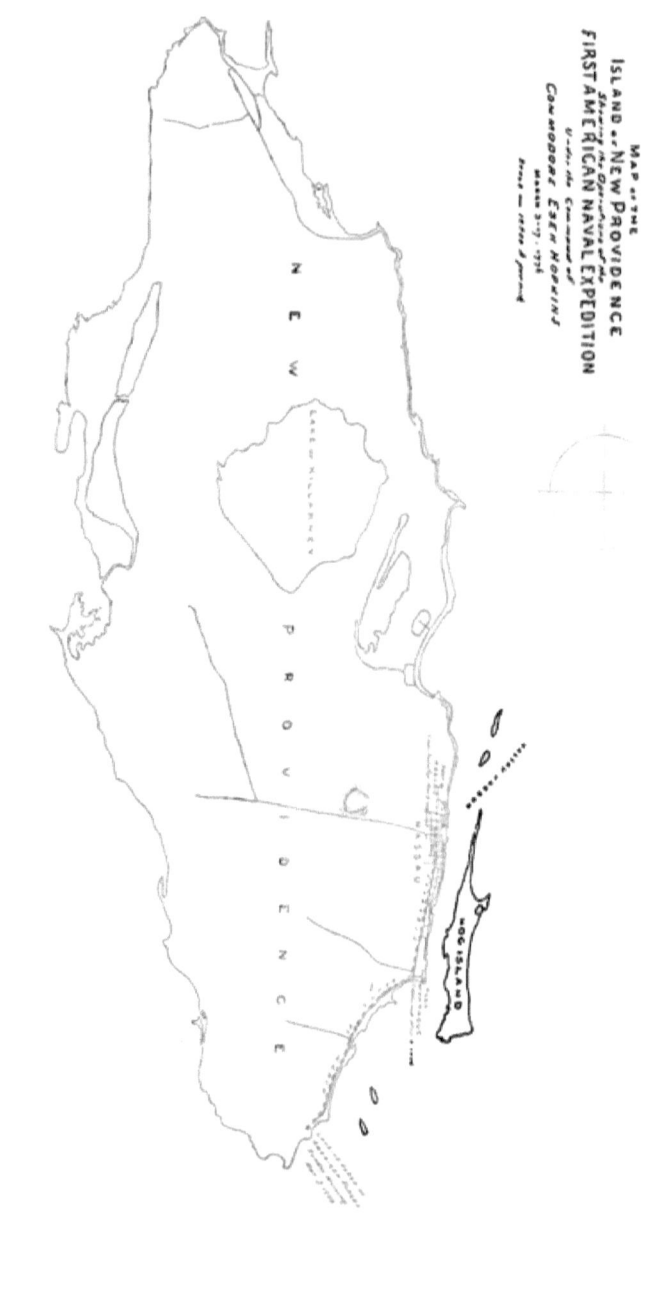

MAP of THE
ISLAND of NEW PROVIDENCE
Showing the Operations of the
FIRST AMERICAN NAVAL EXPEDITION
Under the Command of
COMMODORE ESEK HOPKINS
March 3-17, 1776

Given under my hand on board the Ship
'*Alfred*' March 3rd 1776

ESEK HOPKINS

Cr in Chief" [1]

The next morning the troops marched
upon Fort Nassau, but this pacific measure
had the desired effect, for a messenger appeared from the governor and told Captain
Nicholas that "the western garrison (Fort
Nassau) was ready for his reception and that
he might march his force in as soon as he
pleased." The inhabitants quietly withdrew
from the fort, leaving the governor, Montford Brown, as its only occupant. Hopkins
then dispatched Captain Nicholas to the
governor with an order demanding the keys
to the fortress, which order was complied
with, and the troops at once took possession
of the work and all of its stores. [2]

---

[1] Letters and orders of the Commander-in-Chief.

[2] "*Inventory of Stores &c taken at New Providence at Fort
Nassau*

March 3 1776

71 Cannon from 9 to 32 Pounders
15 Mortars (Brass) from 4 to 11 inches
5337 Shells

A rich store of munition of war rewarded the expedition. So great indeed that it was found impossible to convey it all in the vessels of the fleet, and Hopkins impressed a large sloop called the " *Endeavor*," which he

```
9837 round shot & 165 chain & dble Hd do
 140 hand grenades
 816 Fuzees or false fires
  90 Spunges Rammers & worms
  46 Copper Ladles
 407 Copper Hoops & 5 Copper Powder Measures
 220 Iron Trucks for carriages
   3 Bells
  24 Casks Powder
     A quantity of match rope
   2 dble blocks with brass sheaves
   1 scale beam
   1 Hammer
   3 Tanned Hides
   2 boxes tallow candles
   4 Bbls flower 4 do bread 4 do Beef
     Part of a cask of Spiritt
   1 Sun diall & 1 English flagg
```

Stores taken at Fort Montague

March 3, 1776

```
  17 Cannon from 9 to 36 pounders
1240 Round shott
 121 Shells
  81 Iron Trucks for Carriages
  22 Copper Hoops
   2 Copper Powder Measures
   1 Worm 1 Ladle
     Some old Iron Copper & Lead not weighed."
```

From the original among the Hopkins Papers in the Rhode Island Historical Society.

found in the harbor, for the purpose, promising the owners to send it back and pay for
its use, which was subsequently done. Two
weeks were occupied in transferring the captured property to the vessels, and it was not
until the seventeenth that the fleet got under way for the homeward voyage. In the
meantime, the "*Fly*," which had disappeared
the second day out, made her appearance, and
her commander reported that she had "got
foul of the '*Hornet*' and carried away the
boom and head of her mast." In her disabled condition the "*Hornet*" made her way
to South Carolina, where she safely arrived.
When the fleet sailed Hopkins took away as
prisoners of war, the governor of the island,
Montford Brown, the lieutenant-governor,
and Mr. Thomas Arwin, "Counsellor and
Collector of his Majesty's Quit Rents in
South Carolina," and "Inspector General of
his Majesty's Customs for North America."
Although this expedition had been so successful, yet its one great object had, in a
measure, failed, for the governor, aroused in
his suspicions at the sight of so many formidable vessels approaching the island had,
on the night before the troops landed, loaded
one hundred and fifty casks of powder into

a small sloop and sent her away, thus securing it against capture. Taken as a whole, however, the descent on New Providence was a well planned and a successful exploit.

Hopkins sailed from the Bahamas on the seventeenth[1] of March, and the whole fleet kept in company with the exception of the " *Wasp*," which soon after getting to sea parted from the other vessels.

As the fleet started upon its homeward course Hopkins issued the following order to his captains:

" Orders given the several captains on Sailing from New Providence March 18 1776

SIR: You are to keep company with the ship I am in if possible—but should you separate by accident you are then to make the best of your way to Block Island Channel and there to cruise in 30 fathom water south from Block Island six days in order to join the fleet. If they do not join you in that time you may cruise in such places as you think will most annoy the Enemy, or go in Port as you think fit. and acquaint me by

---

[1] Letter of John Paul Jones to Joseph Hewes. Hopkins Papers, vol. 4, note 10.

the first Opportunity so that you may receive further orders

Ship "*Alfred*" March 18 1776 "[1]

Lieutenant Elisha Hinman, of the "*Cabot*,"
was put in command of the sloop "*Endeavor*," which Hopkins had pressed into
service to assist in the removal of the stores
from the forts, and he was ordered to keep
company with the fleet; in the event of his
parting company, however, he was directed
to use his "best endeavors to get into Providence" (R. I.) "if you cant get in there,"
continued the order, "you are to go in the
East side of Rhode Island, Howlands Ferry
under the Fort, or into New London and
whenever you get into port you are to Land
your guns and stores and send to Governor
Nicholas Cooke at Providence, or Governor
Trumbull for further orders 'till you hear from
me." The material secured was of inestima-
ble value to the colonies and came at a time
when all such munitions were sorely needed.
But the stores secured at Nassau were not
the only fruits of this cruise. Nothing occurred to enliven the voyage homeward until

[1] Orders and Letters of the Commanders-in-Chief," in Rhode
Island Historical Society.

the fourth of April, when the squadron, then
being near the east end of Long Island,
overhauled the schooner "*Hawk*," of the
British fleet, commanded by Lieutenant Wallace, a son of James Wallace, commanding
the fleet at Newport, with whom Hopkins
had already had some experience. This
vessel carried six carriage guns and eight
swivels, and fell an easy prey to her more formidable adversary. The next day " a Bomb
brig the '*Bolton*' of eight guns and two
howitzers ten swivels and forty eight men
well found with all sorts of stores, arms, powder etc." was captured, all of which highly
elated the commander and all the officers and
men in the fleet. All this had been accomplished without the loss of a single man in
action. The next morning, the sixth of
April, about one o'clock, the fleet fell in with
His Majesty's ship, the "*Glasgow*," a heavily
armed vessel of twenty guns, with a comple-
ment of one hundred and fifty men. A tender also accompanied her. By half past two,
the "*Cabot*," Captain John B. Hopkins, had
come so near that he hailed her, and upon
ascertaining who she was immediately fired
a broadside; and now, in the gloom of early
morning, a desperate encounter took place.

The heavy guns of the "*Glasgow*" played upon the "*Cabot*" with such effect that she was so damaged in her hull and rigging as to be obliged to retire for a time from action; besides, her commander and seven men had been severely wounded, and four of her crew killed outright.[1]

Hopkins' own ship, the "*Alfred*," now came into action and for three hours the fight was most severe. While the "*Alfred*" was hotly engaged, the "*Columbus*," Captain Abraham Whipple, ran under the stern of the "*Glasgow*" and raked her as she passed:

[1] A list of the Kill'd & Wounded on board the Brigantine "*Cabot*" Vizt

April 6, 1776

KILL'D

No 1   James Heard Wilson   Lieutenant of Marines
" 2   Charles Sinclair Seymour   Master
" 3   Patrick Kaine   ⎰
" 4   George Kennedy ⎱ Marines

WOUNDED

No 1   John B. Hopkins Esq   Capt
" 2   David Evans   Landsman
" 3   George Britt   Seaman
" 4   James Trowden   ⎫
" 5   Thomas Doyle   ⎪
" 6   Christian Gosner   ⎬ Marines
" 7   John Curtis   ⎭

From the original among the Hopkins Papers in the Rhode Island Historical Society.

the "*Andrea Doria*" sailed into position on
the larboard quarter of the "*Glasgow*," while
the "*Providence*," Captain Hazard, changing
her course occasionally, sent shot after shot
against the British ship. Thus the ships
fought until day began to break, when
" Captain Tyringham Howe, of the '*Glasgow*,' perceiving the force of the American
fleet, seemingly increased by a large ship
and a snow, which kept to windward as
soon as the action began, and discerning
none of Capt. Wallace's fleet to afford him
the prospect of support, very prudently made
all the sail he could crowd and stood in for
Newport." "The bravery of Capt Howe's
behavior," naturally says Gordon, an eminent English historian, " is to be commended.
That he should have escaped from a force so
much superior when united, does not give
satisfaction to the Americans and is imputed
to some failure in conduct or courage on the
side of their commanders." The losses on the
American ships were not great, however, the
" *Cabot* " sustaining the heaviest loss, while
one man on the "*Columbus*" lost an arm.

Lieutenant John Paul Jones thus describes the action in his entry for the day
on the log book of the flag-ship :

" At 2 A. M. cleared ship for action. .
At third glass the enemy bore away, and by
crowding all sail, at length got considerable
way ahead, made signals for the rest of the
English fleet, at Rhode-Island, to come to
her assistance, and steered directly for the
harbour. The Commodore then thought it
imprudent to risk the prizes, &c., by pursuing
farther; therefore, to prevent our being de-
coyed into their hands, at half-past six made
the signal to leave off the chase, and haul by
the wind to join our prizes. The *Cabot*
was disabled at the second broadside, the
Captain being dangerously wounded, the
Master and several men killed. The enemy's
whole fire was then directed at us and an
unlucky shot having carried away our wheel
block and ropes, the ship broached to, and
gave the enemy an opportunity to rake us
with several broadsides, before we were
again in condition to steer the ship and
return the fire. In the action we received
several shot under water, which made the
ship very leaky; we had, besides, the main-
mast shot through, and the upper works and
rigging very considerably damaged; yet it is
surprising that we lost only the Second
Lieutenant of Marines and four men—we

had no more than three men dangerously,
and four slightly, wounded." Hopkins, in
his report of the action to the president of
Congress, says: "We received considerable
damage in our ship but the greatest was in
having our wheel rope and blocks shot away
which gave the *Glasgow'* time to make sail.
I did not think proper to follow as it would
have brought on an action with the whole of
their fleet and as I had upwards of thirty of
our best seamen on board the prizes and
some that were on board had got too much
liquor out of the prizes, to be fit for duty,
thought it most prudent to give over chase
and secure our prizes and got nothing but
the *Glasgow's'* tender. * * * Among the
dead are Mr. Sinclair Seymour Master of
the *Cabot'* a good officer, Lieutenant Wilson
of the *Cabot'* and Lieutenant Fitzpatrick of
the *Alfred.'* The officers all behaved well
on board the *Alfred,'* but too much praise
cannot be given to the officers of the *Cabot'*
who gave and sustained the whole fire for
some considerable time within pistol shot."

The use of liquor on ship board always
annoyed Hopkins. The rules of the service
permitted it to be served as a ration, and
Hopkins was therefore powerless to interrupt

its use as such. Years before this, while
in the merchant service, he had realized
its demoralizing effect on his men, and
while it was the universal custom to serve
"grog" on ship board at eleven o'clock
in the forenoon and at four o'clock in the
afternoon, the rules of the sea forced him
also to comply with the custom, yet it is
said during his long life at sea and ashore
"he totally abstained from the use of intoxi-
cating liquor as a beverage."

Hopkins arrived in New London harbor on
the eighth of April, bringing in his entire fleet,
with the exception of the prize "*Hawk*." He
at once prepared a full report of his cruise to
Congress and dispatched it by John Avery,
Jr., special express. On April 16 this report
was laid before Congress, where it occasioned
a feeling of joyous satisfaction.

The secretary of Congress was directed
to publish a part of it so that the colonies
might be informed of the success of the
enterprise and the worth of the new navy.
John Hancock, President of Congress, on
the next day sent his personal congratula-
tions, together with certain directions of
Congress, in the following letter:

"PHILADA April 17 1776

SIR

Your letter of the 9th of March,[1] with the enclosure, was duly received and laid before Congress; in whose Name I beg leave to congratulate you on the Success of your Expedition. your Account of the Spirit and Bravery shown by the Men, affords them the greatest satisfaction; and encourages them to expect similar Exertions and Courage on every future Occasion. Though it is to be regretted, that the ' *Glascow* ' Man of War made her Escape. yet as it was not thro any Misconduct, the Praise due to you and the other officers is undoubtedly the same.

I have it in charge from Congress to direct, that you send a compleat List and State of the Stores taken and brought from Providence with the sizes &c and that the Cannon and such other of the Stores as are not necessary for the Fleet be landed and left at New London.

The following extract of a letter from Antiguas, I hope will be of Service to you, with that view I send it

[1] This is evidently an error and should be April.

'ANTIGUA March 26 1776. The Third Division of Transports will leave Antigua in a few days, it is said for New York, under convoy of an old East India Ship, mounting 16 guns. There will be six in Number.'

Wishing you the greatest success and happiness I am

Sir

Your most obed & very hble Serv

JOHN HANCOCK, Presdt.

Commodore Hopkins at New London."

The news of Hopkins' success at the Bahamas and his captures on the return voyage, together with the bravery displayed by his fleet in the encounter with a man-of war, was received with delight throughout the colonies.

A contemporary poet commemorated in verse this triumph of Hopkins. Neptune is represented as being greatly disturbed by this affair while he lay

'In dalliance soft and anxious play.'

with his favorite goddess, and directing the winds to go forth and make known who

¹ Hopkins Papers.

dared to shake his coral throne and fill his realm with smoke.

The winds obeyed, and, having witnessed a battle,

> Amazed they fly and tell their Chief
> 'That How is ruined past relief,
> 　And Hopkins conquering rode.
> 'Hopkins!' said Neptune, 'who is he
> That dares usurp this power at sea,
> 　And thus insult a God?'
> The Winds reply: 'In distant Land
> A Congress sits whose martial Bands
> 　Defy all Britain's force,
> And when their floating castles Roll
> From sea to sea from Pole to Pole
> 　Hopkins directs their course.
> And when their Winged Bullets fly
> To reenstate their Liberty
> 　Or scouge oppressive Bands,
> Then Gallant Hopkins, calmly Great,
> Tho' Death and Carnage round him wait
> 　Performs their dread commands.'

The result being that Neptune, in amazement, resigns his trident and crown to Congress, and says, as

> 'A tribute due to such renown,
> These Gods shall rule for me.'" [1]

Hopkins' name was on the lips of all, and all sang his praises, but as the first burst of

---

[1] "Our French Allies," Stone, page 11.

enthusiasm and elation began to fade away
a change took place, and all that he had
accomplished was lost sight of when the
fact was fully brought to mind that he had
allowed the "*Glasgow*" to escape. So intense was the feeling against him on this
account that prejudice took possession of the
minds of the people, and no amount of argument could brush away the feeling that he had
failed at the supreme moment. From this
time a dark cloud began to gather over the
head of Hopkins which was destined to
gradually settle down over him and obscure
a reputation hitherto unblemished. Captain Whipple, of the "*Columbus*," had been
severely criticised by several of his brother
officers in the fleet for his conduct in the
fight with the "*Glasgow*," and, in order to
have his acts inquired into, he demanded a
court martial in a letter which he sent to
Hopkins on the thirtieth of April. In this
letter he details, at some length, the manœu-
vers of the ships on that memorable morning, and gives a more detailed account of
the part he took in the fight. He says:

  " I have had the Honor to serve you in
the last French War and to your satisfaction

I thought, and since my Arrival at Philadelphia was appointed by the Congress to the
Command of the Ship '*Columbus,*' I have
strictly obeyed your Commands and have
done all in my Power for the Honor of the
Fleet to the best of my Knowledge according to your Orders.   The Night that we
fell in with the '*Glasgow*' Man of War, two
of my Lieutenants was on board of the two
Prizes and fourteen of the best Seamen,
when we was running down on the ship
getting in order to Engage and Quartering
the Men in the places of the others that was
out, the '*Glasgow*' suddenly hauling to the
Northward brought me to the Southward
of her and brought her right into your and
Capta. Hopkins Wake. I hauled up for her
and made all Sail with my three Top Gallant Sails, then Captain Hopkins beginning
the Fire and the '*Glasgow*' returning the
same and my being in her Wake and as far
to Leeward as she it Instantly kill'd all the
Wind which put it out of my Power to get
up with her I strove all in my Power but in
vain, before that I had got close enough
for a Close Engagement the '*Glasgow*' had
made all Sail for the Harbour of Newport
I continued Chace under all Sail that I had

except Steering Sails and the Wind being
before the Beam she firing her two Stern
Chaces into me as fast as possible and my
keeping up a Fire with my Bow Guns and
now and then a Broadside put it out of my
Power to get near enough to have a close
Engagement, I continued this Chace while
you thought proper to hoist a Signal to
return into the Fleet I accordingly Obeyed
the Signal and at our Arrival at New
London I found that the report was from
the '*Alfred*' and the '*Cabot*' that I was a
Coward and many other ill natured things
which I say was a false report, if I did not
do my Duty it was not out of Cowardice but
for want of Judgement. I say all the People
at New London look on me with Contempt,
and here, like a Man not serving the Country in my Station. Therefore I having a
Family of Children to be upbraided with
the mark of Cowardice and my own Character now Scandalized thro' the whole Thirteen United Colonies. It is a thing I
cannot bear and if I am a Coward I have
no Business in the service of this Country.
Therefore I desire that there may, by my
own Request a Court Martial be called on
me, and Tried by my Brother Officers of the

Fleet and either acquitted with Honor or Broke for I want no favour, then if I am Broke the Publick will have a right to despise me and reflect on me and my Family, If I have no satisfaction that way I will return you my Commission and thank the Congress for the Service and Curse them that made the false Report, I have never opened my Mouth to any Body concerning the matter, if your Honor had let me come to Newport when the '*Scarborough*' Man of War lay there as I desired I would have convinced the World that I was not a Coward but now it is out of my Power.

Your Humble Servant

at Command

ABRAHAM WHIPPLE.

N. B. Sir, you must observe it was in the Night when we bore down upon the '*Glasgow*', and could not see as if it had been Day light when she altered her Course

A WHIPPLE"

Pursuant to his request a court martial

Since I made my copy of this letter from the original in the Rhode Island Historical Society, some miscreant has mutilated it by cutting out the postscript and signature. (Author.)

was held on board the "*Alfred*," at Providence, on the sixth of May, and he was promptly acquitted of any misconduct.

Captain Hazard, of the "*Providence*," was also the subject of a court martial for misconduct during the engagement with the "*Glasgow*," which resulted in his being relieved of his command, and Lieutenant John Paul Jones was appointed in his stead.

Upon the arrival of the fleet in New London harbor, Hopkins proceeded to dispose of the material which he had secured at the Bahamas. Some of the captured guns were left at New London, in charge of Governor Trumbull, a number were sent by Captain Jennings to Dartmouth, Mass., and the "*Cabot*" carried twenty-six to Newport to be used in the defence of the island. This action of Hopkins provoked much criticism from the authorities at Philadelphia, and was one of the contributing causes of the troubles which later beset him. In a letter to John Hancock, President of the Marine Committee, he seems to have had a foreboding of impending trouble, for he says: "Inclosed you have a copy of Capt Whipples request to me which suppose I shall grant and expect that may bring on some more

Enquiries but do not expect anything which may now be done will mend what is past."

Soon after the fleet arrived in New London Hopkins was visited aboard his ship by General Henry Knox, who, in a letter to his wife,[1] makes some allusion to the personal appearance and characteristics of the commodore. In this letter he says: "I have been on board Admiral Hopkins' ship and in company with his gallant son, who was wounded in the engagement with the '*Glasgow*.' The admiral is an antiquated figure. He brought to my mind Van Tromp, the famous Dutch admiral. Though antiquated in figure he is shrewd and sensible. I, whom you think not a little enthusiastic, should have taken him for an angel only he swore now and then." Brief as the description is it conveys much information regarding Hopkins' personality.

A most deplorable condition existed on board the fleet on account of sickness. The sick men were at once sent ashore and placed in temporary hospitals, seventy-two being sent from the "*Alfred*," thirty-four from the "*Columbus*," fifty-eight from the "*Andrea*

[1] Drake's Life of Knox.

Doria," seventeen from the *"Cabot,"* sixteen from the *"Providence,"* and five from the *"Fly,"* a total of 202.

Hopkins secured one hundred and seventy men from the army, through the direction of General Washington, to replace those he had landed sick, and on the twenty-fourth of April the fleet sailed from New London for Rhode Island. On the way down the coast the *"Alfred"* got ashore on Fisher's Island and had to be lightened before she could be got off; with this delay Hopkins arrived at Providence before the twenty-eighth, where he immediately proceeded to provision his ships and put them in condition for a three or four months' cruise. While thus engaged he received a peremptory order from General Washington to send the men, who had just been assigned to the navy, to New York. A discouraging and disheartening situation confronted him. Upon his arrival in Providence upwards of a hundred men in the fleet were found sick and unfit for duty who had to be landed, and Hopkins says: "there is daily more taken down with some New Malignant fever." Besides this, in return for the twenty-six heavy guns which he had brought to the defence of Newport, Hopkins

expected to receive authority to enlist men
from the troops there located, but almost at
the same time the demand had been made
for the return of the men from the army a
demand had also been made that twenty of
the cannon be immediately sent to Philadelphia. Under these circumstances "modesty
forbade his asking for men," and he writes:
"If I do I am in doubt whether it would be
granted." On the twelfth of May Hopkins
dispatched the sloop *"Providence,"* Captain
John Paul Jones, for New York, to take
back the men he had secured from the
army.

Trouble soon broke out in the fleet over
the neglect or inability of the authorities to
pay the wages of the crews.

All the enlisted men at least had acquitted
themselves with honor, and now that the
cruise was over they were clamoring for
their pay and naturally becoming more and
more impatient as day after day went by without receiving it. This grievance of the men
on the *"Cabot,"* was made known to Hopkins
by a round robin in the following words and
signed by probably most of the sailors and
marines:

HOPKINS COMMANDANT EN CHEF
la Flotte Américaine

From the original in Rhode Island Historical Society's Collection of portraits page
Portrait Plate 3.

"To the Honble Esek Hopkins Esqr

The Humble Petition of the Company of they Sailors and Marines on Board the Brigg 'Cabot' Most Humbly Showeth.

That your petitioners having served faithfully on board the said Brig in defence of America Since her departure from Philadelphia; and her first Cruise being now out They humbly hope that your Hon^r (According to the usual Custom observed on Board Vessels of War) will advance them some money as they are much in want of necessaries which they cannot proceed on another cruise without They humbly hope that your Honor will pardon this Liberty. and impute it to the real necessity which they now Labour under for the want of Cash to procure them what's necessary for their Health & preservation, and your petitioners as in Duty Bound will ever Pray

Please to turn over where you'll see they Subscribers Names are set down," and on the backside of this petition the following names were written in a circle:

"Christian Gosner,   Thomas Gadsly,
Thomas Forbes,   James Wilkeson,
William Osborn,   John Coates,
John Stirlin,   Anthony Dwyer,

Peter Cashinberg,
Matthew McTee,
Andrew Magee,
James McSorley,
Thos Darby,
Michael Third,
Abel Jons
Robert Mills,
James Hall,
Joseph Wayn,
Benjamin Ford,
Richard Sweeney,
Thomas Clark,
Robert Halladay,
Charles Hamet,
Jacob Pony,
Jacob Maag,
Joseph Ravencroft,
Thomas Goldthwaite,
John Harman,
John Hall,
George McKenny,
Thomas Dowd,

James Bowman,
Rudolph Ecling,
Joseph Antonio,
John Roatch,
John Patrick,
Alexander Baptist,
John Little,
John King,
Thomas Charles,
John Bowles,
Michael Thorp,
James Russell,
John Young,
John Curtis,
William Thompson,
Alexander Lowry,
William Small,
Thomas Clarke Senr,
Christopher Reiney,
Lewis Reding,
Robert McFarling,
John Connor,

We They subscribers, impatiently await your Honor's answer."

Sickness and neglect were laying the foundation for much trouble to the commander.

Only two vessels, the "*Doria*" and "*Cabot*," were sufficiently manned to go into service, and both these, on the nineteenth of May,

sailed out of Narragansett Bay on a short
cruise. The "*Alfred*" was disabled and
unfit to go to sea, "she is tender sided
and the most unfit vessel in the whole fleet
for service and her main mast has a olb
shot through it," wrote Hopkins. The
"*Columbus*" and the other vessels were
short handed by reason of sickness and
the heavy drafts made to man those already
at sea. The fleet, as a whole, was therefore practically useless. The hands of
the commander were tied; he had little
authority; there were other causes, too,
operating against him over which he had no
control and which will later appear. It was,
therefore, with some discouragement that he
wrote to Congress: "I am ready to follow
any Instructions that you give at all times
but am very much in doubt whether it will
be in my power to keep the fleet together
with any Credit to myself or the officers
that belong to it—Neither do I believe it
can be done without power to dismiss such
officers as I find slack in their duty."

Before the fleet had arrived in Narragansett Bay from New London the British
fleet, under Wallace, had withdrawn from
Newport, and for the first time in many

years the waters of Rhode Island were free from British war vessels.

It was about this time [1] that Hopkins was summoned to appear before the Marine Committee [2] to answer for breach of orders. A powerful influence was working against him; whether rightfully or wrongly impelled future events will disclose; it was but the beginning, however, of a long chain of troubles and disasters which rapidly followed each other, and from which Hopkins never recovered.

[1] May 14.

[2] At different periods the committee in charge of naval affairs was known as the Naval Committee, the Marine Committee, and the Board of Admiralty.

CHAPTER V

ON the eighth of May, 1776, there was laid before Congress, presumably by the Naval Committee, the whole subject of the operations of the fleet since it had sailed from the mouth of the Delaware the previous February. It took the form, however, as the Journal of Congress describes it, of "the instructions given by the Naval Committee to commodore Hopkins."

Ever since the arrival of the fleet at New London, some weeks before, Hopkins had been the subject of much fault finding, and prejudice was strongly against him. The advantages gained by the seizure of so many valuable munitions of war at the Bahamas did not counteract the dissatisfaction that had been aroused by the escape of the "*Glasgow.*"

Already there had developed in Congress a spirit that was destined to interrupt that harmony so essential to the success of the

cause in which the colonies were then engaged. There was a lack of unanimity
between the three factions into which the
colonies naturally found themselves divided.

It produced jealousies, developing into
political intrigues, and had a tremendous
deterrent influence in every thing with
which Congress had to do. Sectional prejudices were early manifested and later developed alarming conditions. " Politically the
men of Virginia," says Fiske, " had thus far
acted in remarkable harmony with the men
of New England, but socially there was but
little fellowship between them. In those
days of slow travel the plantations of Virginia were much more remote from Boston
than they now are from London, and the
generalizations which the one people used
to make about the other were, if possible,
even more crude than those which English-
men and Americans are apt to make about
each other at the present day.

To the stately elegance of the Virginia
country mansion it seemed right to sneer
at New England merchants and farmers as
'shopkeepers' and 'peasants,' while many
people in Boston regarded Virginian planters
as mere Squire Westerns.

Between the eastern and the middle states, too, there was much ill-will, because of theological differences and boundary disputes.

The Puritan of New Hampshire had not yet made up his quarrel with the Churchman of New York concerning the ownership of the Green Mountains; and the wrath of the Pennsylvania Quaker waxed hot against the Puritan of Connecticut who dared claim jurisdiction over the valley of Wyoming. We shall find such animosities bearing bitter fruit in personal squabbles among soldiers and officers, as well as in removals and appointments of officers for reasons which had nothing to do with their military competence. Even in the highest ranks of the army and in Congress these local prejudices played their part and did no end of mischief."[1] This anti New England feeling was strong even to the degree of bitterness and showed itself in many measures which Congress was called upon to consider. It affected this infant navy and all concerned with it just as it affected the army. Another influence that operated against Hopkins had its origin in one of the acts of Congress which had

[1] The American Revolution, Fiske, Vol. 1, page 244.

been passed almost at the same time a navy
had been projected. This was the authorized fitting out of privateers to prey upon
the ships of the enemy. It cannot be
charged that it was an unwise movement,
for "without the succor that was procured
in this manner the Revolution must have
been checked at the outset," says Cooper,
yet the influence which this measure produced robbed the navy of much of its effect-
iveness.

"The wages paid on the privateers were
from one half to twice as much as Congress
permitted to be paid on the Government
ships which only gave a share of one third
in all prizes taken and one half in the case
of armed vessels while the privateers offered
one half in all cases and occasionally more
when there was extra hazard."

The inducements thus offered on private
ships deprived the government vessels of a
class of seamen most desirable. It also
opened the way for abuses which were
carried on to an alarming extent; for, it
was not uncommon for some of these privateersmen to sell their shares before sailing,
thereby realizing something before they had
actually left port, and, on account of the

greater share in which they would participate, these advancements to the men on
private war vessels were correspondingly
greater than to the crews of the government
ships. Sometimes sailors on the government vessels would receive their advances,
as was the custom, then they would ship on
a privateer, discount their prospective share
and desert to another section to repeat the
offence.

Hopkins exerted all his energies towards
discouraging these privateering expeditions,
arousing much animosity against himself by
so doing, and so widespread had it become
that he was already beginning to feel its effect.

On the thirteenth of December, 1775, the
committee appointed to devise ways and
means for fitting out a navy presented a
report to Congress, recommending that five
ships of 32 guns, five of 28 guns, and three
of 24 guns be fitted for sea; an appropria-
tion was made and a committee appointed
to carry out this measure.

By this resolve of Congress, two of these
ships were to be built in Rhode Island, and
work was begun while Hopkins was at sea
with the fleet; they were yet unfinished
when he returned from his cruise.

The committee of Congress under whose directions these vessels were to be built, appointed a sub-committee to have the immediate charge of building the two Rhode Island vessels, and its members were selected from among the most prominent and influential merchants and ship owners in Providence.

No more representative body could have been found among the men of Providence. Nicholas Cooke, the governor of the colony, a man of wealth and influence; Nicholas Brown, the leading merchant and ship owner, wealthy and of such integrity that when the town's impoverished treasury necessitated the constant borrowing of money from the citizens of the town, one who was asked to loan a small sum on a town note said " no, but I will loan it to Nicholas Brown;" Joseph Russell, of the firm of William and Joseph Russell, merchants and ship owners; Joseph Brown and John Brown, brothers of Nicholas, and business partners; Daniel Tillinghast, another merchant and ship owner, carrying on a large and successful trade with the West Indies, and later Continental agent for the state; John Innes Clarke, and his business partner, Joseph Nightingale, also merchants; Jabez Bowen, the deputy governor, a

man of heretofore unquestioned integrity;
Rufus Hopkins, a son of Governor Stephen
Hopkins "who had attained a high rank
as a nautical commander," and all men who
had served the colony in various important
positions; these were the men against whom
Hopkins was destined to be arrayed in the
performance of his duty.

Two vessels, named the "*Warren*" and
the "*Providence*," were built under the direction of this committee, the former being 132
feet long, the latter 124 feet.

After Hopkins returned to Rhode Island
from his southern cruise, he devoted much
of his time to the work of getting these ships,
which were then well under way, ready for
sea. He frequently sat with the committee
and took part in the proceedings. He was
thus in a position to be well informed as to
how the work was going on.

He soon ascertained that some of the
members of this committee were engaged
in privateering ventures on their own account, and were using their position and
influence to further their own private ends.
It exasperated him greatly, and he openly
accused them of malpractice. Hopkins
afterwards asserted that the "two vessels on

account of this mismanagement, cost twice
as much as the contract price, owing to some
of the very Committee that built the ships
taking the workmen and the stock agreed for
off to fit their privateers, and even threatening the workmen if they did not work for
them."

The friendship that had heretofore existed
between the Browns, with whom he had been
allied years before in his political battles, and
whose vessels he had commanded, was thus
severed, and Hopkins at once antagonized
them with all the fierceness of his nature.
Such a disregard for the public weal at the
very outset of a most desperate struggle was
disheartening, and it touched Hopkins to the
quick. Patriotism seemed to have burned
out and selfish motives had quenched it.

These troubles and criminal charges "bore
hard on the character of the committee as
merchants and as gentlemen" as it is recorded in the committee's records, and they
resented such imputations. Finally the situation of affairs came to the ears of the members
of the Marine Committee, under whose direction the Rhode Island committee was working,
and a sharp letter was sent to the latter committee on May twenty-first, 1776, rebuking

them for their actions. Indignantly they resented the charges, threw up the whole management of the work, and finally turned over the ships to Stephen Hopkins, then a delegate in Congress. This affair aroused much animosity among the parties, and only added fuel to the flame of discontent then burning.

These two ships when turned over to the delegate in Congress were ready for sea but without crews.

Petty jealousies had grown up among the officers in the fleet. While some of them were Rhode Island men there were many from the other colonies, all clamoring for official advancement, and exerting all their influence to attain it. So strong was this that Hopkins strove to avoid becoming entangled in its attendant controversies by overlooking certain irregularities, thereby weakening himself in the estimation of his friends and his opponents. It seems to have been the first evidence of a weakness in his character. " I am very sensible that every officer has his friends " he wrote to his brother on June eighth, " and that has so much weight with me as not to order a Court Martial, although ever so necessary but when the complaint came in writing and that from the

principal officers of the fleet. I wish to
God, and for the good of my country that
no officer in the fleet depended on any friend
but his own merit." Abraham Whipple had
already been severely handled for his conduct with the "*Glasgow*," and had demanded
a trial by Court Martial. Dudley Saltonstall had pursued such a course in the treatment of his men that Kenneth MacCloud,
writing to Hopkins for an assignment to one
of the ships, takes occasion to interject in his
letter "Captain Saltonstall I will not sail with"
while John Paul Jones, on June twentieth, alluded to him, in a letter, as the "ill natured and
narrow minded Captain Saltonstall." An in-
sight into the spirit which pervaded the officers of the fleet may be obtained by the statements in a letter sent by John Paul Jones to
Joseph Hewes, for he says: "It is certainly
for the interest of the service that a cordial
interchange of civilities should subsist between superior and inferior officers; and
therefore, it is bad policy in superiors to
behave towards their inferiors, indiscrimin-
ately, as though they were of a lower species.
Men of liberal minds who have been long
accustomed to command, can ill brook thus
being set at naught by others, who pretend

to claim the monopoly of sense." That he does not refer to Hopkins by this pointed criticism is evident, for in the same communication he writes: " I have the pleasure of assuring you that the Commander in Chief is respected through the fleet, and I verily believe that the officers and men, would go any length to execute his orders. It is with pain that I confine this plaudit to an individual; I should be happy in extending it to every captain and officer in the service. Praise is certainly due to some; but, alas, there are exceptions."

Meanwhile the remaining ships of the fleet lay in Narragansett Bay, with most of their crews in the hospital. Two new ships ready for service swung idly in the stream, with no immediate prospects of crews to man them. Insubordination among the officers was rampant, and this important branch of the service, at a time when it was most in demand, remained practically worthless.

For some weeks after the "instructions" had been laid before Congress the matter was the subject of consideration, and it was not until the thirteenth of June that action was taken to investigate the subject, when Congress ordered Hopkins and Captains

Saltonstall and Whipple to repair to Philadelphia to be tried for breach of orders. On the next day John Hancock, President of Congress, addressed a letter to Hopkins, wherein he says :

"SIR: Notwithstanding the repeated efforts and solicitations of the Marine Board to put the Continental ships upon a respectable footing, and to have them employed in the service for which they were originally designed, they are constrained to say that their efforts and solicitations have been frustrated and neglected in a manner unaccountable to them; and in support of their own reputation, they have been under the necessity of representing the state of their Navy to Congress, and have informed them that there has been great neglect in the execution of their orders ; and that many and daily complaints are exhibited to them against some of the officers of the ships and that great numbers of officers and men have left the ships in consequence of ill usage, and have applied to the Marine Board for redress. These, with many other circumstances, have induced the Congress to direct you to repair to this city * * * As your conduct in many instances requires explanation you will of

course be questioned with respect to your
whole proceedings since you left the city."
Similar letters were also sent to Captains
Saltonstall and Whipple; General Washington was also apprized of the summons to the
three officers of the fleet.

In response to this summons Hopkins
and his two captains repaired to Philadelphia. During the absence of Hopkins the
command devolved upon Captain Nicholas
Biddle, the ranking captain in the fleet.
This officer was without any authority
save on his own ship, and what confusion
and insubordination existed previously was
intensified by the departure of the commander and the two captains. It was not
until September that Hopkins returned. On
the eleventh of July, Saltonstall and Whipple, upon recommendation of the Marine
Committee (the new name for the Naval
Committee), were exonerated by Congress,
Whipple being gently admonished "to culti-
vate harmony with his officers." The trial
of Hopkins, however, was not so soon disposed of, and it was not until August twelfth
that he appeared before Congress. To a
friend, about this time, he wrote: "I am
glad that I am to be tryed by a Court that I

can have no doubt but will judge from matters of fact and not from any rumors propagated out doors without the least foundation."

He certainly expected that he would receive fair treatment in the consideration of his case, and that sectional prejudices and political differences would not be made the basis of the judgment of his superiors.

Hopkins appeared before Congress, and on the twelfth of August, "the examination taken before the Marine Committee," and the report of the Committee were read to him, after which he addressed the delegates in Congress, giving his reasons for pursuing the course he had, and produced two witnesses to substantiate his statements; then he withdrew from the hall.

The main points of Hopkins' defence are outlined in a letter to his brother, written a few days before he was summoned to Philadelphia for trial. In this he says:

"When I went to the Southward, I intended to go from New Providence to Georgia, had I not received intelligence, three or four days before I sailed, that a frigate of twenty-eight guns had arrived there, which made the force, in my opinion, too strong for us. At Virginia they were likewise too strong. In Delaware and New York it would not do to attempt. Rhode Island, I was sensible, was stronger than we, but the force there was nearer equal than anywhere else, which was the reason of my attempts there, which answered no other end than the British force quitting the Government.

When I attempted the fleet at Rhode Island, had all the commanders behaved as well as I expected they would, I should have had it in my power long before this to have relieved most of the Southern Governments from their present difficulties; but as the case was, it was lucky we did not fall in with the whole strength at first. I was not deceived in the strength of the enemy, but greatly in our own resolution; perhaps I was wrong in not giving my sentiments fully at first, the reason of which was, I was in hopes then of some further action, and that we might retrieve the character of the fleet. But the inattention to business of most of the officers, and an expectation of getting higher stations in the new ships, has, as I think, been some hindrance to getting the fleet ready to sail so soon as otherwise it might. I had no apprehension of the cannon being wanted more anywhere else, which was the reason of my delivering them to Governours Cooke and Trumbull.

The very great sickness which then was, and still is, amongst the seamen of the fleet, rendered it impossible to undertake any enterprise for the relief of any colony, although in ever so much distress. All that I have been able to do was, to send the two brigs on a cruise, which I acquainted them (the Naval Committee) with."[1]

He also prepared a brief memorandum of his answer to the report of the committee "that I did during my cruise southward not pay due regard to the tenor of his instructions," which was thus expressed:

"My orders was maid the 5 day of January and I did not sail till the 17th of February which altered the station of the Enemy perticulior as to the strength of the fleet at Virginia and all the ministerial ships lieing North and South Carolina as appears by Letters from the Naval Committee as also it appears to me they Did not expect I should strictly follow the order But my own judgment and prudence according to the last Article in my orders,"

---

[1] Hopkins Papers, vol. 4, note 26.

The report of the Committee and Hopkins' answer to the charges against him then came up for consideration, and his conduct and official acts were fully discussed. John Adams stood up manfully for his defence; he recognized Hopkins' limitations and frankly admitted them; he realized, too, that other influences besides the conduct of Hopkins were working powerfully among his fellow members in Congress.

Besides this Adams had been from the start much interested in the building of a navy, and the result of its first expedition had filled him with a pardonable pride. Writing to a friend soon after Hopkins arrived from the Bahamas, he said: "You will see an account of the fleet in some of the papers I have sent you. I give you joy of the Admiral's success. I have vanity enough to take to myself a share in the merit of the American Navy. It was always a measure that my heart was much engaged in, and I pursued it for a long time against the wind and tide, but at last obtained it."[1] He therefore entered into the defence of Hopkins with a determination that justice should be done him if it lay in his power to accomplish it.

[1] Hopkins Papers, vol. 4, note 9.

Under the date of August twelfth, 1776, John Adams afterwards wrote: "Commodore Hopkins had his hearing; On this occasion I had a very laborious task against all the prejudices of the gentlemen from the Southern and Middle States and of many from New England. I thought, however, that Hopkins had done great service, and made an important beginning of naval operations.

It appeared to me that the Commodore was pursued and persecuted by that anti New England spirit which haunted Congress in many other of their proceedings, as well as in this case and that of General Wooster. I saw nothing in the conduct of Hopkins, which indicated corruption or want of integrity. Experience and skill might have been deficient in several particulars; but where could we find greater experience or skill? I knew of none to be found. The other captains had not so much, and it was afterwards found they had not more success.

I therefore entered into a full and candid investigation of the whole subject; considered all the charges and all the evidence, as well as his answers and proofs; and exerted all the talents and eloquence I had in

justifying him where he was justifiable and
excusing him where he was excusable."

After the trial had ended William Ellery,
a member from Rhode Island, the successor
of Samuel Ward, who had died in Philadelphia while Congress was in session, came
over to Adams and said: "You have made
the old man your friend for life; he will hear
of your defense of him and he never forgets
a kindness."

Such proved to be the case, for many
years afterwards Hopkins visited his friend
and defender under most distressing circumstances, to show his gratitude for the interest
Adams had taken in his behalf.

Congress held the matter under advise-
ment until the sixteenth day of August, and
on that day passed the following resolution:

"Resolved, that the said conduct of Commodore Hopkins deserves the censure of
this house and this house does accordingly
censure him." On the day following the
passage of the vote of censure Hopkins
addressed a letter to the President of Congress acknowledging the receipt of the copy
of the resolve and stating that he would
remain in Philadelphia "to know if they have
any further commands." On the nineteenth

Congress directed him "to repair to Rhode Island and take command of the fleet formerly put under his care."

Hopkins returned from Philadelphia feeling keenly the strictures of Congress; a reputation heretofore unsullied had been attacked, and the representatives of that country he had used his best endeavors to defend, advance and protect, and in whose interest he had staked his life, had smirched it.

Notwithstanding the great pressure that was brought in Congress to dispose of him entirely, John Adams felt that Hopkins had accomplished much and was entitled to better treatment, and he exerted himself to save him from the disgrace of a discharge, and it is certain that without his efforts Hopkins would have then been dismissed from the service. Of the result Adams wrote:

"Although this resolution of censure was not in my opinion demanded by justice and consequently was inconsistent with good policy, as it tended to discourage an officer, and diminish his authority, by tarnishing his reputation, yet as it went not so far as to cashier him, which had been the object intended by the spirit that dictated the prosecution, I had the satisfaction to think that I had not labored wholly in vain in his defense."

Additional information on this subject is derived from the following words of John Adams, written some months before the trial of Hopkins occurred:

"There were three persons at this time who were standing subjects of altercation in Congress, Gen. Wooster, Commodore Hopkins and a Mr Wrixon. I never could discover any reason for the bitterness against Wooster, but his being a New England man; nor for that against Hopkins but that he had done too much; nor for that against Wrixon, but his being patronized by Mr Samuel Adams and Mr R. H. Lee. Be it as it may, these three consumed an immense quantity of time and kept up the passions of the parties to a great height."

John Paul Jones was at sea in the "*Providence*" when he learned the result of Hopkins' trial. This news he doubtless obtained from some ship master who had not been thoroughly informed in the matter. He may however have felt that the result was less harsh than had been anticipated. At any rate, from the "*Providence*" in " N Latitude

37°40' and W. Long. 54°," on September 4,
he sent a letter to Hopkins by the brig "*Sea
Nymph*," Capt. W. Hopkins, saying: "I
know you will not suspect me of flattery
when I affirm that I have not experienced a
more sincere pleasure for a long time past
than the account I have had of your having
gained your cause at Philadelphia in spite of
party. Your late trouble will tend to your
future advantage by pointing out your
friends and enemies. You will thereby be
enabled to retain the one part while you
guard against the other You will be thrice
welcome to your native land, and to your
nearest concerns. After your late shock,
they will see you as gold from the fire, of
more worth and value; and slander will learn
to keep silence when Admiral Hopkins is
mentioned."

On the twenty-second of August the Marine Committee ordered Hopkins to dispatch
four of the vessels to cruise in the neighborhood of Newfoundland, to destroy the fish-
eries and to intercept British merchantmen
bound for the Gulf of St. Lawrence. At
the same time he was authorized to purchase
the "*Hawk*," one of the vessels captured
by him on his way from the Bahamas, fit it

up and rename it the *"Hopkins,"* and send
this vessel with the others to Newfoundland,
and to "hoist his broad pennant on board
any of the vessels." Such a proposition
seems to imply that already the committee
were somewhat ashamed of the way they
had used him, and sought to atone for it by
offering this honor of naming the vessel as
a sop to his wounded feelings, for, as Judge
Staples well says, "Such a compliment is
seldom paid to an inefficient or unfaithful
officer." On account of the lack of seamen
the ships were not sent on this expedition,
"there are so many privateers fitting out
which gives more encouragement to shares
it makes it difficult to man the continental
vessels," wrote Hopkins. The failure of
this expedition to Newfoundland provoked
much criticism from the Committee, and on
the tenth of October, the Marine Committee
addressed Hopkins this letter, wherein he
was ordered upon another cruise:

"Sir:

We learned some time since with
much concern that the expedition we had
planned for you to execute would prove abortive as the ships had gone out a cruizing
under the Struction of Governor Trumbulls

recommendations, with which we cannot be well satisfied, altho, in this instance, we are disposed to pass it by in silence, being well convinced both he and the several Captains meant to perform Service at a time when the Ships were idle.

Supposing, therefore, that you will have been obliged to lay onside the expedition to Newfoundland. We now direct, that you immediately collect the "*Alfred,*" "*Columbus,*" "*Cabbot*" and "*Hampden,*" take them under your command and proceed for Cape Fear in North Carolina where you will find the following Ships of War

The '*Falcon*' of 18 Guns

'*Scorpion*' of 16 Guns

& '*Cruiser*' of 8 Guns

and a number of valuable prizes said to be 40 in number and other vessels under their protection, the whole of which you will make prize of with ease. We understand they have erected a kind of a Fort on Bald Head, at the entrance of Cape Fear river, but it being only manned with a few people from the Ships we expect you will easily reduce it and put the same in the possession of the State of No. Carolina or Dismantle it as may appear best. When you have performed this service you had best deliver to the Continental Agent there such of your prizes as may sell well or be useful in North Carolina others you may convey into Virginia or this place for we dont recommend your remaining in North Carolina for fear of being blocked up there. Perhaps you may receive advice that will render it eligible to proceed further southward to Rout the Enemies Ships at South Carolina & Georgia and if that is practicable you have not only our approbation but our orders for the attempt.

We hope sir you will not loose one single moment after the receipt of this letter but proceed instantly on this expedition.

> We are Sir
>> Your humble Servants
>> ROBT MORRIS
>> WILLIAM ELLERY
>> JOSIAH BARTLETT
>> THO M KEAN
>> RICHARD HENRY LEE
>> WM HOOPER
>> ARTHUR MIDDLETON."

This letter arrived during Hopkins' absence and was delivered to his son, Capt.

---

¹ Hopkins Papers, vol. 4, note 52.

John B. Hopkins, who had been wounded in the encounter with the "*Glasgow*" but was again on duty. He recognized its importance and at once dispatched it by special messenger to his father. He adds, in a memorandum wherein he excuses himself for opening the letter, that "our ship is all ready but manning." For the same causes this expedition also failed, and, so far as it is possible to now judge, the commander was powerless to act. The apparent disregard of these orders by Hopkins only intensified whatever prejudices had been aroused against him in Congress. Changes were being constantly made in the personnel of the Marine Committee, and this committee was the subject of severe criticism for its inactivity. John Jay, on October 11, the day after the order of the Marine Committee was sent to Hopkins, wrote to Edward Rutledge: "What is your fleet and noble admiral doing? What meekness of wisdom, and what tender-hearted charity! I can't think of it with patience. Nothing but more than ladylike delicacy could have prevailed on your august body to secrete the sentence they passed upon that pretty genius. I reprobate such mincing,

little zigzag ways of doing business. Either openly acquit or openly condemn," and this illustrates the general trend of public sentiment regarding this branch of the service.

Hopkins endeavored to put this order of the committee into execution, and exerted all his influence and energies to this end, and a few days later he appeared before the General Assembly of Rhode Island, then in session at Kingstown, "and applied for an embargo till the Continental fleet was manned." He worked diligently with the members to secure the passage of this act, "but failed in getting it by two votes, owing to a number of the members being deeply concerned in privateering." In despair he wrote to the Marine Committee: "I thought I had some influence in the state I have lived in so long but find now that Private Interest Beares more sway than I wish it did," and he adds: "I am at a loss how we shall get the ships manned as I think near one third of the men which have been ship'd and rec'd their monthly pay have been one way or another carried away in the privateers I wish I had your orders when Ever I found any man on board the privateers giving me leave not only to take him out But all the rest of the men; that might make them more Careful of taking the men out of the service of the State."

This power, however, was denied him, but on October twenty-sixth Congress did provide that "privateers could only fly pennants by permission of Continental Commanders," and such private vessels of war were required to show due respect to continental vessels on penalty of loss of commission.

Thus time dragged on, little being accomplished by the fleet, and the spirit of dissatisfaction with the commander growing stronger and stronger, until the early days of December. One disaster after another had occurred to cast odium upon the little American Navy, and it seemed as though the fates had conspired against it and all connected therewith, when, on the seventh day of December, 1776, a British fleet consisting of "about fifty four sail of transports and sixteen sail of men of war," sailed into Narragansett bay around the north end of Conanicut island into the harbor of Newport. On the next day a force of six thousand men landed and took possession of the town. The news was hurriedly sent throughout the colony, and excitement ran high.

With the British fleet and troops holding Newport and the adjacent territory, the American fleet was as completely blockaded within the waters of Narragansett Bay as was the fleet of Spain at Santiago.

On December tenth, Hopkins, from his flag ship, the "*Warren*," then lying five miles below Providence, sent a dispatch to the Marine Committee explaining the situation in Rhode Island, wherein he says:

"Three days ago the English fleet, of about fifty-four sail of transports and sixteen sail men of war arrived in the bay and two days ago they landed, I believe, about 4000 troops, and took possession of the island of Rhode Island, without opposition. The inhabitants of the town of Newport favored their operation, I believe, too much. The Militia are come in, in order to prevent the further operations. I thought it best to come up the river after the fleet was within about two leages of us with the "*Warren*" "*Providence*," "*Columbus*" brigantine "*Hampden*," and sloop "*Providence*." The inhabitants are in daily expectation of an attack on the town of Providence. I have got the ships in the best position of defence we can make them, without they were fully manned, which they

are not more than half. We lay where the
ships cant come up that draw much more
water than we do. If we get the ships manned, shall take some favourable opportunity
and attempt getting to sea with some of the
ships; but at present think we are of more
service here than at sea without we were
manned." The situation in Rhode Island
at this time was a most alarming one. All
of the state troops were called into service,
the fortifications which had been thrown up
all along the bay side were hurriedly manned, and the whole state became a vast
camp confronting the enemy. For nearly
three years the British remained in possession of the town of Newport and the adjacent territory. During this time, conflicts
between the two contending forces were
frequent.

It was not long after the British forces
took possession of Newport that an incident
occurred which brought down upon Hopkins much criticism from the officers of his
fleet, as well as from the people in the state.

Whether he was justly so criticised is
difficult now to decide, yet the incident was
used against him with telling force in the
events which subsequently took place before

Congress, and was brought up again in a
suit at law which followed.

On the second day of January, 1777, at
about one o'clock in the afternoon, while the
"*Warren*" was lying off Field's Point, at
the entrance to Providence harbor, an
orderly from Colonel Bowen, who was
located at Warwick, came on board and delivered to Hopkins a message containing
the information that a British war vessel
was aground near Warwick Neck, about
half way between Providence and Newport.
At this point there had been erected a
battery of two eighteen pound guns and a
permanent garrison established.

When the news was received, the ship
"*Providence*" lay about a mile below the
point, and the sloop "*Providence*" lay against
the Pawtuxet shore, about four miles still
farther to the southward. As soon as Hopkins received this information, he endeavored
to get down the river to investigate the situation. Captain Allen Brown, a pilot, was
at that time on board the "*Warren*." He is
described as "one of the best in the river,"
who, being consulted as to the advisability
of taking one of the ships down to the point
where the grounded vessel lay, informed

Hopkins "the wind was so far westerly and
blowed so hard that the ships could not be
carried down."

Between Field's Point and Warwick Neck
there was then, and there is now, a reach of
circuitous channel "narrow and crooked."
It was within this reach that years before the
"*Gaspee*" had met her fate after grounding
in its dangerous shoals. Hopkins therefore
did not venture with either of the ships, but,
taking the "*Warren's*" pinnace with twenty-
two men, went to the "*Providence*" (sloop),
Captain Whipple, taking Captain Brown,
the pilot, with him. Upon arriving on board
the sloop and finding her fully manned, they
immediately got under weigh and proceeded
down the river toward the stranded vessel.
As the sloop drew down upon her it was discovered that she was the Frigate "*Diamond*,"
and that she lay "on a shoal which runs off
S. W. from Patience about half a mile from
that Island and a little more S. E. from
Warwick Neck." There was about eleven
feet of water at low tide, and as the tide was
about half down she did not careen. Lying
about a mile and a half off, about south-
west by south, was a fifty gun ship with her
top sails loose, her "anchor apeak," which,

as the wind was, could have floated her within pistol shot of the "*Diamond.*"

Hopkins was of the opinion that on account of the severity of the wind she did not "come to sail." From his knowledge of the river and bay, with the gale then blowing, he felt that it would be unwise to order his ships down to the "*Diamond,*" and even if the wind had not blown so hard and the ships could have been brought down, he afterward said he should not have done so, for "the Enemys ships could have come to sail with any wind that we could and a great deal better as they lay in a wide channel and we in a very narrow and very crooked one." Arriving off Warwick Neck, Hopkins went ashore to the fort, where he was informed by Colonel Bowen that he had sent for two eighteen pounders, and, after remaining there a half hour, until the guns arrived, Hopkins went back to the sloop.

What subsequently took place is best told in Hopkins' own words:

"I went aboard the sloop and we dropped down under the ships stern a little more than a musket Shot off it being then a little after sunset, we fired from the sloop a number of shot which she returned from her stern chasers;

the ship careened at Dusk about as much as
she would have done had she been under
sail, after they had fired from the shore
about twenty six shots they ceased and soon
after hailed the sloop and said they wanted
to speak with me. I went ashore and was
informed they were out of Ammunition. I
offered them powder and stuff for wads but
we had no shot that would do, they sent to
Providence for powder and shot and I went
aboard the sloop and sent some junk ashore
for wads, soon after they hailed again from
the shore and I went to see what they
wanted, and gave Capt. Whipple orders not
to fire much more as I thought it would do
but little execution it being night and could
not take good aim with the guns. When I
got ashore the officer that commanded them
desired that I would let them have some
bread out of the sloop which I sent the boat
off for but the people not making the boat
well fast while they were getting the bread
she drifted away and I could not get aboard
again. The ship by Lighting got off about
2 o'clock the same night."

Hopkins did not regard this exploit with
much concern until nearly two months afterwards, when he found that a "scandalous

account" of the affair had been sent to the Marine Committee by a Mr. Vesey, one of the prize agents at Boston. It so happened that this Mr. Vesey, while on his way from Philadelphia to Boston, stopped at Providence to consult with Hopkins, and when the news that the frigate was ashore reached the "*Warren*" he was on board. Desiring to participate in the adventure he "went down as a volunteer with the Commodore on the sloop '*Providence*,'" and thus became an eye witness to all that occurred. In his account he says: "she (the '*Diamond*') was suffered to depart though the wind was directly down the river so that none of the English ships could come to her assistance."

This story of Vesey's was repeated from one to another and finally became a subject of such importance that it entered largely into the causes which finally led to Hopkins' discharge from the navy.

The officers in the fleet inimical to Hopkins made light of it, the people of the state, who were in no position to know the merits or demerits of the case, roundly censured him for letting a helpless British frigate escape. It served also to bring back again to the minds of all the unfortunate affair of

the "*Glasgow*," while many a smile was produced at the ludicrous position of the commander of the navy rowing backward and
forward from his temporary flag-ship at the
whim of a military officer at a bay side battery, until he lost his boat and was unable to
gain his ship.

Troubles which were growing greater and
greater seemed following closely after Hopkins.

During the early part of the winter the
"*Alfred*" and "*Cabot*" got to sea and succeeded in getting around to Boston, from
which place they cruised independently.
About this time Hopkins wrote to William
Ellery, then a delegate in Congress from
Rhode Island: "We are now blocked up by
the enemys fleet the officers and men are
uneasy, however I shall not desert the cause
but I wish with all my heart the Hon Marine
Board could and would get a man in my
room that would do the Country more good
than it is in my power to do, for I entered
the service for its good and have no desire to
keep in it to the disadvantage of the cause I
am in."

This uneasy, inactive life of the officers in
the fleet, was productive of no good to any

one. Bickerings and contentions occurred between themselves, while it also afforded a favorable opportunity for the completion of a well laid plot to get rid of their commander. It would be unfair to accuse all the officers of the fleet of being parties to this transaction; there were many who were loyal friends of the commander, but among the officers of the "*Warren*," Hopkins' own ship, he seems to have had few whom he could call such.

These events practically close Hopkins' career in the naval service of the United States. The fleet never again got to sea, and, although individual ships performed most valuable and important service, and the officers won imperishable renown for bravery and heroic conduct, the naval squadron, which sailed so proudly on its course from Delaware bay nearly a year before, practically ended its life in Narragansett bay.[1]

---

[1] What ultimately became of all the vessels of the first American fleet is uncertain. No record has been preserved of the fate of the "*Columbus*," "*Hornet*" and "*Fly*." The "*Alfred*" was captured by the "*Ariadne*" and "*Ceres*," in 1778. The "*Cabot*" was driven ashore on the coast of Nova Scotia by the "*Milford*," in 1777, and abandoned. She was afterwards hauled off and taken into the British navy. The "*Andrea Doria*" was burned in the

12

CHAPTER VI

DURING the time that the fleet was shut up in Narragansett Bay, and while Hopkins was exerting himself to find men to man his ships, and struggling against all the opposition with which he had been constantly confronted, a scheme was set on foot to strike him a final blow and crush him completely. He was too active in some respects, if he was charged with inactivity by those who were far removed from the scenes of his labors. In the rearrangement of the navy list, in October, 1776, a law was passed regulating the rank of the officers of the navy and a list of twenty-four captains approved. No special appointment or

Delaware, in 1777 to prevent her falling into the hands of the enemy. The "*Providence*" (sloop) was taken in the Penobscot, in 1779. The "*Wasp*" is supposed to have been sunk in the Delaware to prevent capture by the enemy. The "*Providence*" (ship) was captured at Charleston in 1780, and the "*Warren*" was burned in the Penobscot in 1779. (Naval History of the United States, Cooper, vol. 1, page 247.)

confirmation of the former appointment was
made respecting the Commander-in-Chief.
Hopkins held this position by virtue of his
first appointment, and although each of his
old captains and some new ones received a
special assignment of rank, his name and
rank were omitted. He was not popular
with Congress, and a way was left open,
when the proper time should arrive, to dispose of him entirely, and at the same time
provide against future troubles by making
no provision for such an officer. The time
for such action soon came. It will be remembered that the committee of Rhode
Island merchants and ship owners who had
the charge of building the two vessels in that
state, the "*Warren*" and "*Providence*," had
so far advanced in their work that in the
early spring of 1776 these vessels were
launched.

This committee, in addition to other duties and responsibilities, had the power to
appoint officers for the two ships. This was
a duty not easy to perform. There was no
lack of good men in the state for the service, but government service was not to their
liking, it was less remunerative than that
on private vessels of war, and some of the

very men on this committee were more interested in having their own privateers offi-
cered and manned than they were to serve
their country's interests. This feature was
one of the most troublesome with which
Hopkins had to deal. The privateers took
nearly all the available men, and the government ships were left with insufficient crews.
It will also be remembered that he endeavored to secure from the legislature of
the state an embargo until his vessels were
manned but did not succeed in so doing. He
did succeed, however, in arousing much opposition against him by the owners of these
privateers, and they did not forget his interference. In order to secure officers for the
ships, sub-committees were appointed from
the general committee, to go into the various
towns in the adjoining states and pick up
such men as they could find who would enter
the service. These committees visited the
towns of Boston, Dartmouth, Mendon, Bridgewater, Taunton, in Massachusetts, and other
places, and secured men evidently competent
to assume the duties of the offices to which
they were subsequently appointed. Among
the men thus selected were John Grannis,
Barnabas Lothrop, Samuel Shaw, James

COMMODORE HOPKINS.

Engraved for Murray's History of the American War, & c.
and printed for T. Robson, New Castle-upon-Tyne.
From an original print.

Portrait Plate 1.

Sellers, Roger Haddock, John Truman,
James Brewer, John Reed and George Stillman. There was yet another, Richard
Marvin by name, who was a ship carpenter
and had worked on the vessels now about to
be put in commission. These men were all
assigned to the "*Warren*," on which subsequently flew Hopkins' broad pennant. The
most conspicuous of these men in the plot
which afterwards developed were Marvin and
Grannis. Little is known of John Grannis,
though he belonged in Falmouth, Mass., and
was appointed captain of marines, June 14,
1776. It appears, however, that he was a
willing tool of Marvin's, and from his rank
lent some force and importance to the part
which he was called upon to perform.

Marvin, however, is better known, for in the
latter years of his life he kept a private school
in Providence, and had a large number of pupils, the author's grandfather being enrolled
among them. Richard Marvin was born in
England, in 1750, and was, therefore, a young
man when he entered the service of the colonies; he was by trade a ship carpenter, he
had received more than an ordinary education, was a fine penman, and there seems to
be good reason for belief that he had served

in the British navy, or merchant service, in a subordinate capacity, where he had obtained some knowledge of seamanship and navigation. He received his appointment of third lieutenant on the " *Warren*," from the committee appointed to build the two ships, on April 30, 1776. He was granted a pension on April 4, 1818, "for eleven months actual service as a lieutenant in the U. S. navy" during the Revolutionary War. After the war Marvin took up his residence in Providence, where he lived until his death, June 17, 1826. He was constantly employed in the ship yards, and on the public works of the town, until the early part of the present century, when he gave up his trade and opened a school for boys, on Pawtuxet street, now Broad street, opposite to Fenner street, which school was well attended. While he always signed his name " Richard " he was known far and wide then, and even to-day is referred to as " Dicky Marvin." He is described by one who remembered him well, as " a large, fat man, marked in his personal appearance as in his mental peculiarities;" another calls him a " peculiar character;" and another an " old time eccentric character," while one of his old pupils says,

"Marvin was a very profane man, and a great reader of Thomas Paine." The concensus of opinion of this old sailor man and pedagog pictures him as an irascible, meddlesome man, profane and vulgar in speech and habits. He was, however, a good schoolmaster, and insisted on discipline, which he enforced with a birch switch; he was also a most skillful penman and made this study interesting for his pupils by writing doggerel rhymes for them to copy. The author holds among his treasures an ancient copy book formerly belonging to his grandfather, used while a pupil of Marvin's, which bears ample testimony to his qualifications as a penman. There is a deal of humor, as well as reason, in some of the rhymes which Marvin "set for copy." A boy who was not prompt in his appearance at the regular hour for opening school, would find written in an elegant hand on his copy book:

"When you are sent to school set out and run
Dont stop to play nor join in idle fun
But lay your course, port helm, and brace away,
And soon you'll land in Marvin's peaceful bay."

All of Marvin's rhymes seem to have had a nautical flavor. Among his pupils was James West, who was learning the trade of a caulker. He worked part of his time in the shipyard, and received instructions from Marvin during his spare moments. Mr. West, in after years, well remembered this verse which his preceptor set for him to copy:

"Be wise and be industrious Jeams,
And drive the oakum smartly in the seams,
Be faithful in your labors, for on you,
Depends the lives of seamen, the ship, and Cargo too."

Such was the man who became the ringleader in a miserable conspiracy to rob Hopkins of his good name, and to force his removal from the command of the American navy. How well this conspiracy succeeded, future events will disclose.

Long before this scheme was set on foot Hopkins had aroused the ill will, if not the enmity, of many of the influential merchants in Providence, by his efforts to stop the sailing of privateers. It will be remembered that he had gone before the legislature and endeavored to have an "embargo laid upon Privateering in order that the Continental ships might be manned." His sensational charges against the foremost men of Providence, who constituted the committee to build the two war vessels, had produced

much feeling against him, and the disorder
with which this committee had terminated
its career shows plainly enough that the
members were angered and embittered by
his interference.

There was a spirit of unrest, too, among
the officers and men in the ships at this
time, and the opportunity of using this condition to the detriment of Hopkins was taken
advantage of by some of the men whom he
had antagonized. It was, evidently, determined that certain charges should be made
against him by such officers in the fleet as
were unfriendly to their commander. Who
these men were cannot now be definitely
stated. Hopkins refers to them in a letter
to William Ellery as "some of the Gentlemen of this Town, (Providence) I suppose
the owners of the Privateers, who I am
sorry to say are greatly prejudiced against
me."

With this substantial backing of men of
such influence and wealth it was an easy
matter to enlist the sympathies of these idle
and restless men in the fleet in any proposition to attack the commander.

This attack came from the ship "Warren,"
on which Hopkins had hoisted his broad

pennant, and came in the form of a petition
to the Marine Committee.

Early in February, 1777, this petition was
drawn up and quietly circulated among the
officers on the "*Warren*," and it was subscribed to by Roger Haddock, John Truman,
James Brewer, John Grannis, John Reed,
James Sellers, Richard Marvin, George Stillman, Barnabas Lothrop, and Samuel Shaw.
Some of the officers to whom it was presented, however, refused to attach their
names to it.¹ All these men, with the exception of Marvin and Haddock, were residents of Massachusetts, Marvin being the
only Rhode Island man among them, and he
a resident of Providence. Haddock belonged
in New York, and was master of the "*Warren*;" Truman was a gunner, and Brewer a
carpenter, both of Boston; Grannis was captain of marines, and belonged in Falmouth;
Reed was the chaplain, and belonged in Middleborough; Sellers was second lieutenant
of marines, and came from Dartmouth;
Stillman was first lieutenant of marines,
and came from Barnstable, as did Lothrop,
who was a second lieutenant of marines;

¹ See Proceedings of Court Martial of R. Marvin, page 207.

Shaw was a midshipman, and belonged in Bridgewater. This petition, to which these men subscribed their names, was as follows:

"ON BOARD THE SHIP '*Warren*,'

Feb 19. 1777.

Much Respected Gentlemen:

We who present this petition, engaged on board the ship '*Warren*' with an earnest desire and fixed expectation of doing our country some service. We are still anxious for the Weal of America & wish nothing more earnestly than to see her in peace & prosperity. We are ready to hazard every thing that is dear & if necessary, sacrifice our lives for the welfare of our country, we are desirous of being active in the defence of our constitutional liberties and privileges against the unjust cruel claims of tyranny & oppression; but as things are now circumstanced on board this frigate, there seems to be no prospect of our being serviceable in our present station. We have been in this situation for a considerable space of time. We are personally well acquainted with the real character & conduct of our commander, commodore Hopkins, & we take this method not having a more convenient opportunity of sincerely & humbly petitioning, the honorable Marine Committee that they would inquire into his character & conduct, for we suppose that his character is such & that he has been guilty of such crimes as render him quite unfit for the public department he now occupies, which crimes, we the subscribers can sufficiently attest.

P. S. Capt Granis the bearer of this will be able to give all the information desired.

> Roger Haddock
> John Truman
> James Brewer
> John Granis
> John Reed
> James Sellers
> Richard Marvin
> George Stillman
> Barnabas Lothrop
> Samuel Shaw[1]

To the honorable Marine Committee"

Besides this general petition all of its signers subscribed to separate papers in

---

[1] From a copy of the original laid before Congress. See also Hopkins Papers, vol. 3, page 10.

which each made specific charges against
the commander.

By these Hopkins was charged with profane swearing in common conversation, curs-
ing the Marine Committee and calling its
members as well as Congress itself "ignorant
fellows—lawyers clerks—persons who dont
know how to govern men:" his conduct in
the management of the fleet was also com-
plained of. The most temperate of all these
individual charges was that of John Reed,
the chaplain, and on account of some of its
statements is important in arriving at a just
conclusion as to what there was in the miserable scheme.

Reed's testimony against his commander
was as follows:

"ON BOARD THE '*Warren*.'

Feb. 24. 1777

I the subscriber do know that our commander, commodore Hopkins, allows himself to speak in the most disrespectful manner concerning the honorable Continental
Congress, although I have lived in the cabin
with him, I do not remember that he has
ever once spoken well of those guardians of
America, but seems to embrace every opportunity in order to disparage & slander them.

He does not hesitate to call them a pack of
ignorant fellows — lawyers clerks — persons
that don't know how to govern—men who
are unacquainted with their business—who
are unacquainted with the nature of mankind—that if their precepts & measures are
complied with the country will be ruined.   I
have also heard him say that he would not
obey the Congress. He not only talks about
them most disrespectfully among our own
folks but I have heard him exert himself
earnestly in order to disparage them before
strangers, before two prisoners who were
masters of vessels on their passage to Newport in order to be exchanged. He also pos-
itively asserts that all mankind are exactly
alike—that no man ever yet existed who
could not be bought—That any person living could be hired with money to do any action whatsoever. This he also asserted in
the hearing of the before mentioned prisoners, for what reason I can't determine unless
he was desirous of making a bargain with
Sir Peter Parker.

He allows himself in anger & in common
conversation to take the name of God in
vain; he is remarkably addicted to profane
swearing. In this respect as well as in many

other respects he sets his officers & men a
most irreligious & impious example. He
has treated prisoners in the most inhuman
and barbarous manner—I very well know by
hearsay, how he has conducted in regard to
his men's being paid off & being discharged
when the term of time for which they engaged
was expired. In this part of America people are afraid of him. They are jealous of
him & he is an effectual obstacle to the fleets
being properly manned. He is very much
blamed by people here for not destroying a
British frigate when aground a few days ago
in this river. I am not prejudiced against
the man. My own conscience, the regard I
have for my country and the advice & earnest desire of many respectable gentlemen
have induced me to write what I have written.

JOHN REED."

As soon as the signatures had been obtained these documents were intrusted to
Captain John Grannis, who, without so much
as asking leave of absence, quietly deserted
the ship and set out for Philadelphia to

1 From a copy of the original laid before Congress. See also
Hopkins Papers, vol. 3, page 14.

present the petition to the Marine Committee. Hardly had Grannis left the "*Warren*," when Shaw, Reed and Haddock, who had signed the petition, appeared voluntarily before Hopkins and frankly admitted they had signed a petition to the committee derogative to him, and confessed that they had been induced to do so " by some Gentlemen of the town." Further inquiry brought Hopkins the information that Grannis was missing from the ship without leave and the names of some of the signers. With this information he at once addressed a letter to William Ellery, a delegate in Congress from Rhode Island, in which he says:

" I have lately understood by two or three officers of the ship "*Warren*," who came voluntarily to me; that they had been Induced to sign some paper or Petition greatly to my disadvantage: which they were perswaded to by some of the Gent.ⁿ of this Town, I suppose the Owners of the Privateers, who I am sorry to say are greatly prejudiced against me, since I endeavoured to get an Embargo laid upon Privateering in order that the Continental ships might be mann'd—And as for Captn. Grannis who I understand is gone to you with it, I am

well perswaded he never has been on board
the ship three nights together, nor I believe
ten days this five months past—and all that
he can have against me as we are entire
strangers, is that after several times desiring
him to go on board and do his duty, as the
ship was liable to be attack'd at any time; I
at last threaten'd to break him and get
another man in his Room if he did not—
upon which he went on board but staid only
two nights—and this single thing must Con-
vince every Impartial Person, that for an
officer of a Ship to leave her without the
knowledge of the Captain or Lieutenant,
when she was in danger of being attack'd
every day being within ten miles of some, &
twenty of ten or twelve Men of War, some
of them stronger than her, two hours fair
Wind would have brought them along side;
and to go such a Journey without first en-
deavouring to Remedy the Evil if there was
any, cannot be a Friend to his Country, but
must act upon some private View, which
I make no doubt he did to serve some of
the men perhaps that made him, much in
the same manner as they finished the Ships,
who have cost your Agent near if not quite
£4000—which was absolutely necessary for

them before they could be ready for the
Sea—and that you will soon be convinc'd
off by his accounts, which he says you
will have soon and they are near if not
double the Prices first Contracted for, owing
to some of the very Committee that built the
Ships, taking the Workmen and the Stock
agreed for, off to work and fitt their Privateers ; and even threatning the Workmen
if they did not work for them—I am very
willing to come to you to answer for my
Conduct with such of the Committee who
built the Ships as I could name—but not
with the poor men who only acted as Ma-
chines to a Sett of Men who I wish I could
say I thought had any other principle but
avarice—and it would have been full as well
if some of the Officers had brought in such
accounts for Enlisting men, that they might
have been Settled with on any other Terms,
but signing that Paper against me. And it
will be well if you don't find them Extrava-
gant, as the Committee did not chuse to pay
them, but gave em Orders on the Agent for
the Money—

Inclosed you have a Copy of one of the
Officers accounts—and I believe you will
find in the Committees account whenever it

comes to hand, another large sum and all for
Enlisting men; but few of whom ever came
on board the Ships, though I can't Say they
did not go on board the Privateers—Whenever I am call'd for I think I can Speak the
Truth, and not Stab a man in the dark—

What the purport of the Complaint which
Capt Grannis may have brought is, I do not
know, but as the Men that Sign'd it know
but little, and are worth less as Sailors, all I
shall say more is to Inclose a Copy of what
three of them Voluntarily Sign'd being Con-
scious they had done wrong—

This one thing I can Say, and with Truth,
that I engag'd in this dispute on no other
design than to serve my Country—and I
still am determined not to desert the Cause
—but whenever you or the Congress think
you can get a man in my room that will be
of more service to the Cause than I can, you
have my leave, and in Justice to the Country
I think you ought to do it—and I shall still
Continue to do what good I can, in a less
Envy'd and less troublesome way ."[1]

Grannis proceeded to Philadelphia and
upon his arrival promptly appeared before
the Marine Committee with the scurrilous

[1] Letters and orders of the Commander-in-Chief, page 74.

documents which had been entrusted to
him. Even with the prejudice which the
members of the committee had against
Hopkins the allegations contained in the
papers presented were too serious to be at first
believed. After deliberating over the whole
matter for some days it was resolved to sum-
mon Grannis before the committee and examine him personally as to the charges that
he and his fellow officers had made. A sub-
committee was appointed to "examine John
Grannis on the subject matter of the petition."
The testimony before this committee was not
under oath, Grannis merely answering the
questions put to him by the committee.

After the usual questions as to his name,
residence and occupation, the examination
proceeded as follows:

" Q. Are you the man who signed the
petition against Esek Hopkins, Esq by the
name of John Granis.

A. Yes.

Q. Do you know the other subscribers
to said petition

A. Yes

Q. Are any of them officers of the
'Warren,' & if officers what office do they
sustain

A. John Reed is chaplain & belongs to Middleborough & James Sellers is Second Lieutenant of the '*Warren*' & of Dartmouth. both of Massachusetts Bay Richard Marvin is third Lieutenant & of Providence George Stillman first Lieutenant of Marines, Barnabas Lothrop Second Lieutenant of Marines both of Barnstable, Samuel Shaw is a Midshipman of Bridgwater Roger Haddock is master of the frigate & formerly was of New York, & John Truman is gunner. & James Brewer Carpenter & both of Boston in the State aforesaid.

Q. Have you a personal acquaintance with Esek Hopkins Esq

A. Yes. I have had a personal acquaintance with him since I came on this ship

Q. Did you ever hear him say anything disrespectful of the Congress of the United States & what & when.

A. I have heard him at different times since I belonged to the frigate speak disrespectfully of the Congress have heard him say, that they were a set or parcel of men, who did'nt understand their business, that they were no way calculated to do business, that they were a parcell of lawyers clerks, that if their measures were followed the country

would be ruined & that he would not follow
their measures. I have heard him say the
above in company on ship board & words to
the same effect on shore. Sometimes the
above was spoken of Congress in general
but more frequently of the Marine Committee.

Q. Did you ever hear him speak disrespectfully of Congress or the Marine Committee before prisoners.

A. No I never was in his company when
prisoners were present.

Q. Do you know anything about his
treatment of prisoners

A. I was on board the frigate 'Providence,' when there were about 20 prisoners
on board. They were called into the cabin
where I was & were asked by Capt. Whipple, whether they would do ship's duty.
They answered No. Capt. Whipple said
it was his orders from the Commodore to
put them in irons, to keep them on two
thirds allowance & by God, he would obey
the commodore's orders. They were sent
out of the cabin with an officer who returned
& said he had put them in irons. There
were also some prisoners sent on board the
frigate 'Warren,' who were forced to do

ship's duty by commodore Hopkins' orders & he refused to exchange them when a cartel was settled & other prisoners were exchanged. but don't know that it was their turn. The reason he assigned for not exchanging them was that he wanted to have them enlist on board the frigate

Q. Do you know anything about a British frigate, being aground last winter in the river or bay leading up to Providence in the State of Rhode Island &c. and what.

A. I did not see the '*Diamond*' frigate while she was on shore in Jan last I was then on board the '*Warren*,' which with the Continental fleet lay just above a place called Field's Point Commodore Hopkins went down the river in the sloop '*Providence*' & sometime after he returned. I heard him say that the people in Providence blamed him for not taking the '*Diamond*,' but that the men were not to blame, for they went as far as he ordered them & would have gone further if he would have permitted them, but that he did not think it safe to go with the sloop, for that the '*Diamond*' fired over her I heard a number of people who said they were at Warwick neck, when the '*Diamond*' was aground there, say, that commodore

Hopkins was so far off the ship, that his shot did not reach her, that the ship lay so much on a careen, that she could not bring any of her guns to bear upon the sloop; and further I heard some American seamen who were prisoners when the *Diamond* was aground say, after they were exchanged, that the ship lay so much on a careen, that they could not have hurt the Sloop's people so long as they kept out of the reach of her small arms. They also said, that it was the intention of the enemy to have fired the ship & left her if the sloop had come near enough to have played upon her. One of the seamen who told me the above was ― Weeks, & another of them was named Robinson Jones both of Falmouth aforesaid & young men of good general reputation

Q. Were the frigates manned when you came from Providence.

A. No. There was then about 100 men on board the '*Warren*,' & I heard some of the officers of the frigate '*Providence*' say, that in last December they had on board about 170 men & the last of February I heard them say, that so many of their men were dead & ran away, that they were then not better off for men than the '*Warren*.'

Q. Commodore Hopkins is charged with being a hindrance to the proper manning of the fleet, what circumstances do you know relative to this charge

A. For my part his conduct and conversation are such that I am not willing to be under his command. I think him unfit to command & from what I have heard officers & seamen say, I believe that it is the general sentiment of the fleet & his conversation is at times so wild & orders so unsteady that I have sometimes thought he was not in his senses & I have heard some others say the same. And to his conduct & conversation it is attributed both by people on board the fleet as well as by the inhabitants of the State that the fleet is not manned. It is generally feared by the people both on board the fleet as well as ashore, that his commands would be so imprudent that the ships would be foolishly lost, or that he would forego opportunities of getting to sea or attempt it, when impracticable. The seamen belonging to the *Columbus* left her when their time of service expired & went into the army & I heard some of them say that they would not enlist again into the Continental fleet so long as Commodore Hopkins had the command

of it. The character that Commodore Hopkins bore was a great hindrance to me in
getting recruits.

Q. Had you liberty from Commodore
Hopkins or Capt Hopkins to leave the frigate you belong to.

A. No I came to Philadelphia at the
request of the officers who signed the petition against Commodore Hopkins & from a
Zeal for the American cause.

Q. Have you, or to your knowledge either
of the signers aforesaid any difference or dispute with Commodore Hopkins since you or
their entering into the service.

A. I never had, nor do I believe that
either of them ever had. I have been
moved to do & say what I have done &
said from love to my country & I very
believe that the other signers of the petition
were actuated by the same motives." '

This testimony being committed to writing
was signed by Grannis. It was not until
March twenty-fifth that the committee was
prepared to lay the matter before Congress,
but on that day the Marine Committee "laid
before Congress a paper signed by sundry

From a copy of the original laid before Congress. See also
Hopkins Papers, vol 3, page 15.

officers in the fleet containing charges and complaints against Commodore Esek Hopkins."

These papers were read and the whole matter laid upon the table. The next day (March twenty-sixth) the matter was taken up, and without any discussion it was " Resolved, That Esek Hopkins, be immediately and he is hereby, suspended from his command in the American Navy."

About this time, while Hopkins was harrassed by the contentious spirits around him, he learned that his son Esek, a young man nineteen years of age, was a prisoner of war at Halifax. Young Esek Hopkins had graduated from Rhode Island College in the class of 1775 and almost immediately entered the navy as a midshipman, and was assigned to the "*Alfred*," the flag-ship. He rapidly rose to the position of lieutenant, and while acting in this position on the "*Providence*" (sloop) he was captured by the British and taken to Halifax. Through the influence of his father the General Assembly passed an act requesting Major General Spencer, then in command of the Continental forces in Rhode Island, to exchange Lieutenant Otway, of the British frigate "*Lark*," who had been

captured by the state troops, for the son.
No such exchange, however, took place, for
young Hopkins sickened and died while a
prisoner in the hands of the enemy. He
was a young man of much promise, and his
father, no doubt, felt his loss keenly.

Meanwhile extraordinary proceedings were
taking place in the fleet. Hopkins was incensed at the underhanded and improper
manner in which the complaint of his sub-
ordinates had been brought to the attention
of Congress. As the head of the navy he
had been ignored and insulted, and he resented it squarely.

Before Grannis had reached Philadelphia
the whole plot to deprive Hopkins of his
command and put a blot on his reputation
had been exposed. The master of the
"Warren," Roger Haddock, chaplain Reed,
and midshipman Shaw, who had come to
realize the enormity of their acts, presented
themselves before their commander and ac-
knowledged their offence; at the same time
each subscribed to a document very different
in tone to that which had been entrusted to
Grannis for the perusal of the Marine Committee.

Hopkins closely questioned the three men

and ascertained the true state of the whole
business. He learned that the plot had originated outside of the fleet, and that the men
on board the "*Warren*" had been easily
drawn into the scheme through the influence of the erudite Marvin. It is interesting to observe the difference in the
declarations made by Haddock, Reed, and
Shaw, after they had confessed their part in
the plot, from those to which they had previously subscribed their names. Haddock's
was in the following words:

"Ship *Warren*' March ye 16 1777

I the subscriber do hereby say that I know
nothing either of the public or private character of Commodore Hopkins as being a
stranger, nor know not that he has done
anything detrimental to the cause he is now
engaged in at Present

ROGER HADDOCK.

Witness DANL. TILLINGHAST"

Reed subscribed to the following:

" This may certify

That I the subscriber in my own person
have been treated complacently by Commodore Hopkins & don't know that he has

designedly acted in any one instance inimically to his country but that according to the best of his abilities, suppose that he has acted consistently therewith

PROVIDENCE 14 March 1777   JOHN REED

Witness at Signing   SAM LYON." [1]

While Shaw put his name to the following statement:

"These may certify

That I, the subscriber have been treated by Commodore Hopkins since I have been in the navy with the greatest politeness and decency and never have thought that he has been inimical to his country designedly, but has according to the best of his abilities acted consistent therewith

SAMUEL SHAW

PROVIDENCE March 14 1777

Witness at Signing   SAM LYON."

For some days after Hopkins had obtained the information of this attack upon him he devoted himself to quietly investigating the matter. During this time he ascertained that Lieutenant Richard Marvin, of the "*Warren*," had been the prime mover in circulating

Hopkins Papers, vol. 3, page 14.

the scurrilous documents about the ship,
and that his relations with certain men in
the town gave color to the suspicion that he
was the ringleader in the plot. Hopkins
therefore placed him under arrest, and on
the third day of April, 1777, he was tried by
court martial held on board the "*Providence*," then lying near Fields Point, in
Providence River, for circulating a "scurrilous paper or papers signed by him and sent
away in a private manner against the Commander in Chief."

This Court consisted of Captains Abra-
ham Whipple, John B. Hopkins, Hoysted
Hacker, Jonathan Pitcher, Silas Devoll and
Joseph Hardy, and Lieutenants William
Grinnell, Robert Adamson, William Barron,
Philip Brown, Adam W. Thaxter, Seth
Chapin[1] and Edward Burke. The Court
organized with Abraham Whipple president,
and Marvin was presented and asked if he

[1] Seth Chapin, was the son of Ebenezer and Abigail (Perry)
Chapin, and was born in Mendon, Mass., March 31, 1716. He
married for his first wife Elizabeth Rawson, of Mendon, October
27, 1707; she died, November 17, 1775. On October 10, 1776,
he married Eunice Thompson, of Medway, Mass. He had nine
children, four sons and five daughters. From 1756 to 1791, he
held the office of town clerk of Mendon, and was a Deacon in the
Congregational Church.

was ready for trial. Upon answering " Yes,
—I am ready" he was then sworn and examined as follows:

Capt Whipple   Q. " Did you ever Sign
any paper or Petition against the Commander-in-Chief or against any officer in the
Fleet to be sent to Congress

A. Yes—

During the war of the Revolution, Seth Chapin served with distinction. He was corporal in Captain John Albees' company,
which marched on the Lexington alarm April 19, 1775, from
Mendon to Roxbury, and served nine days.

December 10, 1775, he was a corporal in Captain Job Taylor's
company of Colonel Joseph Read's regiment.

July 9, 1776, he was second Lieutenant in Captain Samuel Crag-
in's First Company of the Third Worcester County regiment.
Previous to this, on June 24, 1776, he was appointed Second
Lieutenant of Marines on board the ship "*Providence*," and on
September 14, 1776, he was ordered to Plymouth, Mass., to enlist
men for the navy.

He did not serve long in the marine corps, for in the same year,
he served as First Lieutenant of Wood's Regiment of the Massachusetts militia. On December 8, 1776, he was commissioned Lieutenant in Captain Samuel Cragin's Company, Lieutenant Colonel
Nathan Tyler's regiment ; he was discharged, January 21, 1777.

July 10, 1777, he was First Lieutenant in Colonel Sherburn's
additional continental regiment which commission he resigned
April 19, 1780.

His most daring exploit was on the night of December 17, 1778,
when, in a small boat with six men, he captured a British brig in
the Seaconnet river. He also carried on secret communication
with Isaac Barker, a farmer in Middletown, R. I., while the British
held possession of Newport and the island of Rhode Island. Barker, who was a staunch patriot, lived at his home in Middletown,
and was in the midst of the British forces, indeed British officers

Q. Will you produce the Copies of such Papers as you have Signed and Sent to this Court

A. They are not in my possession and if they were I would not

Capt Whipple Q. Why did you not at the time you sent those papers inform the Commander in Chief or Captain Hopkins [2] of it

were quartered at his house, but by signals which he made by arranging his bars at a gateway, he was enabled to convey information to Chapin, who was located at Little Compton, R. I., across the Seaconnet river, which was of the greatest importance to the Americans. This was carried on successfully for nearly fourteen months, or until the British evacuated Newport.

From official muster rolls it appears that he was commissioned 1st Lieut. 19 July, 1777, in Capt. James Webb's Co., Col. Henry Sherburne's Regt. Rolls for Jan. 21 to Aug. 21, 1778; Nov., 1778; Jan.-Apr., 1779; and was 1st Lieut. Capt. James Webb's Co., Col. Henry Sherburne's Regt., for July and Aug., 1778 Roll dated at camp at R. I., 21 Aug., 1778, reported on guard. Lieut. in Col. Benj. Hawes Regt. for service at R. I.; detached July, 1778; engaged Aug. 2, 1779; discharged Sept. 12, 1779. Roll of Capt. Baker's Co. dated at Upton. Served as Lieut. 1m 15d. in Capt. Cragin's Co., Col. Hawe's Regt. at the time the enemy landed on the Island; and 1m. 15d. as Lieut. in Capt. T. M. Baker's Co. during Sullivan's expedition, in 1778. 1st Lieut. in 1st Co., Capt. Phil. Ammidon, 3rd Worcester Regt., commissioned 27 Aug. 1779. Lieut. of 3d Worcester Co. Regt. (no date). Lieut. in Capt. Phil. Ammidon Co., Nathan Tyler's Regt.; enlisted 27 July, 1780; discharged Aug., 1780; marched on alarm to R. I. 27 July, 1780; commissioned Capt. in Regt. to be raised for 3m. service, July, 1780.

[2] John B. Hopkins was at this time captain of the "*Warren.*"

14

A. Because the act of Congress Says we shall quietly and decently make the same be known to our Superior Officer

Q. Did you Sign any Paper against any other Officer but the Commander in Chief—

A. I have no answer to make to that

Q. How many was there that Signed those papers with you against the Commander in Chief

A. The Congress can make that known

Q. What was the reason you did not acquaint the other officers in the Fleet of it as they might have Signed the Petition or other papers which you have Sent to Congress

A. Because we thought they were not so thoroughly acquainted with the Facts, that we Sent to Congress as we were

Q. Was any person in Providence or within this State directly or Indirectly at that time knowing of any such Petition being Sent to Congress

A. I believe there was

Q. What is their names—

A. Their names will appear to a greater Advantage hereafter

Q. Who was the first promoter of drawing & sending this Petition

A. I cannot tell distinctly

Q. Was Henry Marchant Esqr[1] consulted in drawing this Petition

A. I am not certain—

Capt Hopkins Q. What was the Contents of the Petition Sent to Congress against the Commander in Chief

A. The facts were of such a nature that we thought it was our duty to our Country to lay them before the Congress

Commodore Hopkins Q. What Country was you born in

A. I was born in England, but america is grown dear to me

Q. Was there any more Signed the paper or Petition besides Yourself

A. Yes there was—

Q. How many do you think there was

A. I cannot give you a direct answer

Capt Whipple Q. Would you tell how many Signed it if you did know

A. If I knew exactly I would

Q. Will you tell the number that you know Signed it—

A. Have I not answered a Similar Question put to that already

Capt Hopkins Q. What did you ever

---

[1] Henry Marchant was a delegate to the Continental Congress from 1777 to 1780, and from 1783 to 1784

See in the Commander in Chiefs Conduct
that gave you any cause to Sign and Send
any paper to Congress against him or did
he ever treat you or any Officer on board
with any disrespect to your knowledge—

A. Some thing that I thought was injurious to the publick Wellfare—

Commodore Hopkins Q. What was it
that ever I did that was Injurious to the
public Wellfare—

A. A number of Facts coming to our
knowledge which we thought was our duty
to Submit to Congress

Q. Do you remember what the facts
were

A. I do remember

Capt Whipple Q. If you remember will
you tell what they were

A. Whenever Congress or any body
authorized by them, calls upon me I am
ready to relate the Facts

Q. Do you think you was acting in the
character of an officer when you made &
Signed a Complaint and sent it away privately
against your Superior Officers—

A. I think I was—

Capt Hopkins Q. do you (personally)
know of any Fact you ever Saw that the

Commander in Chief committed which you have signed and sent to Congress

A. I refuse answering to that until such time as I appear before Congress or a Committee authorized by them to inquire into the affair

Mr Adamson Lt. of the 'Warren' was asked the following Questions:

Commodore Hopkins Q. Was you not asked to Sign that paper that Capt Grannis carried to Congress

A. Yes

Q. What was the reason you did not

A. My reason was that the Facts mentioned against the Commander I did not know to be true.

Commodore Hopkins Q. Do you know any of the facts charged against me

A. You was charged with saying that there was no man but what could be bought and that the Congress was made up of Merchants, Clerks, Lawyers, and Boys

Q How many do you Understand Signd the Petition

A. Eight

Mr Thaxter to Mr Marvin

Q. Was the Chief mate of the 'Warren' asked to sign the Petition against

Commander Hopkins that was sent to Congress

A.   I don't know that he was

Capt Whipple   Q.   Was there any Complaint Sent away with the Petition against any other Officer or by those belonging to the '*Warren*'

A.   None that I know off—

Capt Whipple   Q.   Have you anything to say to the Court in your own defense

A.   I have nothing very material"[1]

Upon the conclusion of this trial the Court recorded the opinion that Marvin had "treated the Commander-in-Chief of the American Navy with the greatest indignity, and defamed his character in the highest manner by signing and sending to the Honorable Continental Congress several unjust and false complaints against the Commander-in-Chief in a private and secret manner, and also violating the 28th 29th and 31st Articles for the Regulation of the American Navy, which they think is acting beneath an officer of his station."

The Court also rebuked him for the

---

[1] From the original record of the court martial in Hopkins Papers, vol. 3, page 2.

insulting manner in which he had conducted himself before it, and for this considered him "unworthy of holding a commission in the American Navy." The order of the Court was, "that Lieutenant Richard Marvin forthwith deliver up his commission to the Commander in Chief—and in case he should refuse to do it that he be put under immediate Confinement until he comply with the Resolve of this Court."

On the same day the findings of the Court were confirmed by the Commander-in-Chief.

Marvin's career in the American Navy terminated with this act. He had received his appointment as Lieutenant on April 30, 1776, and on April 3, 1777, he was dishonorably discharged. For these eleven months' service, much of which time he had devoted to breeding discontent among his associates and indulging in underhand methods against the Commander of the Navy, he afterwards received a pension from the United States.

News and the post travelled slowly in those days. More than a week before this court martial had convened Congress had suspended Hopkins from his command in the Navy, yet he was as ignorant of it as though such an order had never been passed.

It was not until the fifteenth day of April that he was notified of the action of Congress, but on that day Daniel Tillinghast, Continental Agent for Rhode Island, at half past two o'clock in the afternoon, placed in the hands of Esek Hopkins a copy of the order suspending him from his command, certified and attested by John Hancock, president. Without a hearing, without the privilege of saying one word in his own defence, and without so much as the formality of a trial, the Commander-in-Chief of the Navy had been summarily suspended from his command and his good name had been assailed. Such proceedings, however, had not been without precedent. Others high in official position had been thus served, and others were destined to feel the keen darts of insult. To a man of Hopkins' temperament, who had for years been accustomed to rule, who was working earnestly and fearlessly in a cause in which he had enlisted heart and soul, the action of Congress came with crushing force; a weaker character would have succumbed with the shock. Hopkins, however, was made of sterner stuff.

About the time that Hopkins received the

formal order of his suspension he also received a letter from his friend William
Ellery, then representing Rhode Island in
the Continental Congress, in which he expressed his regret at the action of that body.
To this letter Hopkins responded on the
20th of April. Notwithstanding the great
injury that had been done him and the humil-
iation which his suspension had brought, this
letter shows the manly spirit with which he
received this verdict and his undiminished
patriotism. Thus he writes:

" PROVIDENCE, April 20th 1777—

To THE HON WILLM ELLERY ESQ.

*Member of the Contl Congress, at
Philada.*

SIR I receiv'd your esteem'd Favour of
Town meeting day just time enough to get
chose a deputy for this Town.—had I receiv'd it a Week sooner perhaps I might
have been at the head of the Prox—

Altho' I have lost the Interest of a parcel
of mercenary merchants Owners of Privateers, I do not think I have lost it in the
Major part of this State—I heartily wish the
Fleet may do well in the way you have directed it—I am obliged to you for your

advice to continue a Friend to my Country, and you may depend I shall, should I have a few Friends in it—neither do I expect to remain Inactive—

I can assure you it gives me great Satisfaction that in my own judgment I have done everything in my power (or would have been in any other mans power in my place) for the Service of my Country—One thing I must ask, and shall think I am not well us'd if it is not granted— That is an attested Copy of a paper or petition Sign'd by some of the Ship *Warrens'* Officers, and perhaps some other men to the hon. Marine Board, or to Congress—Should it be in your power to obtain it please to send it soon—if not, please to let me know the reason why I am not to be allow'd it—and you will much oblige

Sir

Your real Friend

ESEK HOPKINS."[1]

In compliance with this request for a copy of the petition which had been sent to Congress, a resolution was passed, on May 14, directing that a copy of the complaint made

[1] Hopkins Papers, vol. 1, page 77.

by the men on the "*Warren*" be delivered
to Mr. Ellery for the use of Hopkins. He
repeatedly requested that this order of Congress might be complied with, and it was
not until several months afterwards that he
received these copies and learned exactly the
charges that caused his suspension.[1] Hopkins remained under suspension until January 2, 1778, when he was summarily
dismissed from the service of the United
States. It is sometimes stated that he
refused to appear before Congress after he
had been suspended and answer the charges
made against him, and for this neglect Congress rebuked him; there does not appear,
however, any evidence to substantiate this
statement. The scheme of his enemies had
succeeded, he was no longer in the way, the
nefarious plot of a few skillful men had prevailed. Smarting under the sting, and
knowing that he would receive no consideration from Congress, he determined to have
justice done him in a court of law. He
therefore consulted with Rouse J. Helme, a
leading attorney of the state, a man of great

---

[1] The last official letter recorded in the Orders and Letters of
the Commander-in-Chief of the Navy is dated July 4, 1777, and
is a request to William Ellery for a copy of these charges.

influence and activity in its affairs, and it
was decided to bring a suit for criminal libel
against the officers who were concerned in
the conspiracy, with damages laid at £10,000.

This suit was begun by a warrant issuing
out of the Inferior Court of Common Pleas,
of Rhode Island, on January 13, 1778, directing the sheriff of the county of Providence
to arrest the bodies of Roger Haddock, John
Truman, James Brewer, John Granis, James
Sellers, Richard Marvin, George Stillman,
Barnabas Lothrop, Samuel Shaw and John
Reed, and have them before said court on
"the third monday in June" following.

This warrant was placed in the hands of
Martin Seamans, sheriff, who subsequently
made return of service on Samuel Shaw and
Richard Marvin, the other parties, defendants, doubtless being without the jurisdiction
of the court.   Both these men gave bail, the
former presenting Ebenezer Sprout, of
Middleborough, Mass., the latter furnished
John Brown, of Providence.   It is significant
that the leader in the conspiracy, who had
been dishonorably discharged from the Navy
for his participation in the scheme, found a
sponsor in the person of one of the members
of the very committee that Hopkins had

charged with malfeasance in office, and which
committee it was alleged had instigated the
charges to deprive him of his command.
This case was heard at the June term of the
Inferior Court of Common Pleas, to which the
writ had been returnable. Soon after being
arrested on the libel suit, Marvin and Shaw
presented a petition to Congress, representing that they had been made defendants in
a suit—that they were without the means to
defend themselves and were put to much
trouble and charge, and asked Congress
to defray the expense of their defence.
This petition was considered by Congress,
and on the thirtieth of July an act was
passed giving them the relief prayed for, and
on the next day the following letter from
Henry Laurens, president of Congress, was
sent to the petitioners transmitting a copy
of the act of Congress:

" PHILADELPHIA 31st July 1778

GENTLEMEN Inclosed with this you will
receive an Act of Congress' of the 30th inst

"¹ IN CONGRESS JULY 30 1778.

The committee to whom was referred the petition of Richard
Marvin and Samuel Shaw brought in a report which was taken
into consideration whereupon

Resolved, that it is the duty of all persons in the service of the

for defraying the reasonable expenses of
defending the suit against you by Capt Esek
Hopkins, together with attested copies of
the records of Congress respecting his appointment & dismission to & from a command in the Continental navy

I am Gentlemen

Your most obedient servant

HENRY LAURENS Presd of Congress

P. S. inclosed is a duplicate of the Act
of Congress of the 30th, which if necessary
you will deliver to the Inferior Court

Messrs Richard Marvin & Samuel Shaw
Providence"

United States as well as all others the inhabitants thereof, to give
the earliest information to Congress or other proper authority of
any misconduct, frauds or misdemeanors committed by any officers
or persons in the Service of these States. which may come to their
knowledge

Whereas a suit has been commenced by Esek Hopkins Esq
against Richard Marvin & Samuel Shaw for information & complaint by them & others made to Congress against the said Esek
Hopkins while in the service of the United States

Resolved that the reasonable expenses of defending the said suit
be defrayed by the United States.

Ordered that the Secretary of Congress furnish the petitioners
with attested copies of the records of Congress, so far as they
relate to the appointment of Esek Hopkins Esq to any command
in the continental navy and his dismission from the same, and also
to the proceedings of Congress upon the complaint of the petitions
against the said Esek Hopkins, presented to Congress through
the marine committee as mentioned in their petition."

With this substantial backing and with
the effect it produced the defendants came
before the court for trial. Marvin and
Shaw secured for counsel William Chan-
ning, Esq., of Newport, then attorney general of the state. Hopkins produced as
witnesses to testify to his character and conduct men eminent in the community, men
who had known him for years on shore and
at sea; they were: Capt. Joseph Olney;
the Rev. James Manning, a Baptist clergyman, and at this time president of Rhode
Island College; Captain Daniel Tillinghast,
the Continental agent for Rhode Island;
Captain Ambrose Page, a sea captain, a
member of the General Assembly of Rhode
Island, and afterwards Judge of the Admiralty Court of Rhode Island; and Stephen
Potter.

The trial of this case occupied five days.
Captain Joseph Olney, the first witness for
the plaintiff, was engaged, and in his examination testified:

"Question. Captain Olney, are you acquainted with Esek Hopkins Esq. character
as a public officer & a private gentleman, if
so please to relate his character.

Answer. When he commanded the fleet

I always looked upon him as a commander always desirous to serve his country & in the fleet we looked upon him as a gentleman

Question. How long have you been acquainted with Mr Hopkins and what time did you enter the service on board the fleet which commodore Hopkins commanded.

Answer. I entered on board the fleet under his command at Philadelphia in December 1775 and remained there all the time he commanded it. My acquaintance with him has been from my youth up.

Question. Have you ever heard the conduct of commodore Hopkins as commander of the fleet censured.

Answer. I have heard his conduct blamed by some in Philadelphia & in particular Mr Newman and Capt Shaw who left the fleet at New London.

Question. Have you heard that the public in general censured the conduct of Commodore Hopkins while he had the command of the fleet.

Answer. I have heard him censured but by them that I thought knew nothing of the affairs of the fleet.

Question. On board of what vessel was

Robert Hopkins, Esq.
Commodore of the AMERICAN Sea Forces

From an original print ... ...
America, ...

Portrait Plate s

you an officer, and was you with the said Esek Hopkins the whole of the time he had the command of the fleet.

Answer. I was Second Lieutenant on board the 'Columbus' until he returned from Philadelphia, & then was appointed to the command of the 'Columbus' until January 1776.

Question. Did you ever hear Esek Hopkins Esq speak disrespectfully of the Congress or the Cause we are engaged in

Answer. No."

Rev. Dr. Manning was then sworn and examined, testifying in reply to the questions put to him as follows:

" Question. How long have you been acquainted with Esek Hopkins Esq & what is his general character.

Answer. From more than seven years intimate acquaintance with said Esek Hopkins Esq., I have had the highest reasons to esteem him a man of honor & respectable character amongst mankind & a zealous advocate for the cause & liberty of his country & disposed to serve it with his best abilities.

Question. Have you ever heard the

15

conduct of the said Esek Hopkins as commander of the fleet censured.

Answer. I have heard many say that he
ought to have gone out with the fleet before
the Enemy came to Newport, and others
justified his bringing the Ships into the river,
but whether they were qualified from personal knowledge of the state of the fleet,
to form a judgment, I am not able to say.

Question. Are you acquainted with the
conduct of the said Esek Hopkins Esq while
on board the fleet.

Answer. No"

Daniel Tillinghast's testimony disclosed
another point of the libel not heretofore
mentioned in the case, and the insinuation
that he had been irregular in his transactions
with his men regarding prize money met
a prompt denial. Tillinghast's testimony
being as follows:

"Question. Are you acquainted with Commodore Hopkins & for how long, and what
is his general character as an officer, seaman
and gentleman in private life.

Answer. I have been personally acquainted with Commodore Hopkins above
28 years & have always (   ) him to be an

experienced officer & much of a gentleman
in a private character.

Question. Did Commodore Hopkins
receive the wages & prize money belonging
to the seamen under his command in the
fleet.

Answer. No.

Question. As the British fleet arrived in
the river & at Newport was the fleet under
the command of commodore Hopkins fitted
for sea, were they after the arrival of (   )
British fleet finished & a considerable sum
of money expended on them

Answer. I having a personal knowledge
of the situation of the fleet at that time,
know they could not proceed to sea, and a
considerable sum of money was expended
on the Ships after the fleet arrived.

Question. Did Commodore Hopkins ever
call on you as Continental agent to pay off
the seamen & make division of the prize
money.

Answer. He did & I paid as long as I
had any money in my hands.

Question. Do you conceive the conduct
of commodore Hopkins to be any way detrimental to maning said fleet.

Answer. I did not.

Question. What number of men had they on board the ship '*Warren*' & the other ships.

Answer. To the best of my knowledge about 110 and but few seamen. among them on board the '*Warren*'. on board the '*Providence*' about 100. & the '*Columbus*' about 30. the Sloop '*Providence*' about 15 —

Question. Are you acquainted with the conduct of the said Esek Hopkins when on board the fleet. Did you ever hear his conduct censured by the public

Answer. As to his conduct while on board the fleet I never heard but he behaved as an experienced officer, nor was I on board to see his conduct. I have heard him censured often by people that I was sure did not know the situation of the fleet at that time "

The examination of Captain Ambrose Page, who had known Hopkins from his boyhood days, was of much the same character as that given by others and was submitted as follows:

" Question. Are you acquainted with the character of Commodore Hopkins as an officer, seaman and as a gentleman in private life, please to relate.

Answer. I have known Capt Esek Hopkins Esq from his youth, until he commanded the American fleet, to my certain knowledge his character as an honest judicious commander ever has been esteemed amongst the gentlemen of this town. I have also known him in the W Indies on several voyages, where he was much respected by the merchants of my acquaintance, & I doubt not but every gentleman will allow him, a sincere friend in the cause of his Country

Question. Did you ever hear the conduct of the said Esek Hopkins Esq. as commander of the fleet, censured & by whom.

Answer. I do not particular remember, but some of the then present council did not justify his not going to sea on the expectation of the British fleet taking possession of Newport.

Question. Are you acquainted with the conduct of Esek Hopkins Esq. while commander & on board the fleet.

Answer. No.

Question. As you was one of the members of the upper house of Assembly when commodore Hopkins requested the advice of the Committee who acted in the recess of the General Assembly, what was to be done with the fleet under his command as the British fleet then a vast deal superior in numbers & force were approaching what was the answer given by Commodore Hopkins.

Answer. As near as I remember, was this. His orders was on his being fitted & manned to go on a second expedition therefore could not proceed to Boston as we advised, but if he could take any measures to man his fleet; would immediately proceed to Sea"

In concluding the evidence in the case for the plaintiff Stephen Potter made the following deposition in open court:

" The deposition of Stephen Potter Esq duly sworn saith that he had been acquainted with Commodore Hopkins & that he the Said Hopkins hath borne the character of an honest man as far as I ever knew or heard, & I have been acquainted with him for near twenty years & I never heard him charged with any thing criminal that disqualifies him in my opinion from serving in any station whatever. I have heard some persons fault him in some matters, that when they had done, I concluded they were not judges of; they were matters of his staying in Providence river with the fleet."

The depositions of the three officers who had first warned Hopkins of the conspiracy were also submitted.

The defendants relied almost entirely for their case upon the proceedings in Congress. Full copies of all the acts of Congress relative to Hopkins' connections with the navy had been transmitted by the secretary of that body, as well as copies of letters from President John Hancock and others, to the Commander; there were also the depositions of the officers and men on the "*Warren*" who had signed the petition to Congress against Hopkins, as well as copies of the petition and complaint itself. In addition to the depositions of the officers of the "*Warren*" heretofore presented in the narration of the events leading up to this point, there were submitted to the court those of Sellers, Marvin, Stillman, Lothrop, Brewer and Truman, and, that an impartial review of the case may be made, they are here given.

These depositions accompanied the petition and complaint when it was first sent to Congress, and were as follows:

"ON BOARD THE SHIP 'Warren'

February 23. 1777.

The regard which I have for my country has induced me to write the following accusations against commodore Hopkins:

First. I know him to be a man of no principles & quite unfit for the important trust reposed in him. I have often heard him curse the honorable Marine committee in the very words following ' God damn them. they are a pack of damned fools If I should follow their directions the whole country would be ruined. I am not going to follow their directions, by God.' Such profane swearing is his common conversation, in which respect, he sets a very wicked and detestable example both to his officers & men. 'Tis my humble opinion, that if he continues to have the command, all the officers who have any regard to their own characters will be obliged, very soon, to quit the service of their country. When the frigates were at Newport, before the British fleet took possession of that place, more than an hundred men who were discharged from the army. the most of them seamen, were willing to come on board the ships and assist in

carrying them to Boston, or any other harbor
to the Eastward, in order that they might be
manned, but Commodore Hopkins utterly
refused, being determined to keep them in
this state, from which we have not been
able after all our pains to procure a single
man for this ship. He has treated prisoners
in a very unbecoming barbarous manner.
His conduct and character are such, in this
part of the country that I can see no prospect of the fleet ever being manned.

JA'S SELLERS."[1]

"Ship 'Warren' Feb. 24 1777.

The following lines contain the reasons
why we signed the petition against commodore Hopkins. We consider him on account
of his real character, quite unfit for the important public station wherein he now pre-
tends to act. We know him to be, from his
conversation & conduct, a man destitute of
the principles both of religion & morality.
We likewise know that he sets the most impious example both to his officers & men by
frequently profaning the name of Almighty
God & by ridiculing virtue. We know him
to be one principal obstacle or reason why

[1] From a copy of the original laid before Congress. See also
Hopkins Papers, vol. 3, page 14.

this ship is not manned & people are afraid
to engage in the fleet through fear of their
being turned over to this ship. We have considered it as an indispensible duty we owe
our country sincerely to petition the honorable Marine Committee, that his conduct
& character may be inquired into, for as
things are now circumstanced we greatly
fear these frigates will not be in a situation
capable of doing America. any service

> RICHARD MARVIN
> ' GEORGE STILLMAN
> BARNABAS LOTHROP

Commodore Hopkins is very much blamed
by people here for not destroying a British
frigate when aground a few days ago in this
river, and we suppose very justly

> JAS SELLERS
> RICHD MARVIN" [1]

" SHIP '*Warren*' Feb 24, 1777

I the subscriber have heard commodore
Hopkins say, that the Continental Congress
was a pack of ignorant lawyers clerks & that
they knew nothing at all. I also have heard
him say, when earnestly persuaded to remove

---

[1] Hopkins Papers, vol. 3, page 14.

the fleet to Boston, being in constant expectation that this river would be blocked up.

The ships shall not go to Boston, by God.

JAMES BREWER"[1]

"Ship *Warren* Feb 24 1777.

I the subscriber can attest that our commander Commodore Hopkins has spoken
very abusively concerning the Honorable
Congress calling that respectable assembly.
who ought to be considered as the guardians
of American liberty, a pack of ignorant lawyers clerks who know nothing at all

JOHN TRUMAN"[2]

The result of this trial was unfavorable to
Hopkins, for the jury, seven of whom were
residents of Providence, after considering the
evidence, brought in a verdict for "the defendants and their costs," thereby declaring
that the defendants did not "wickedly mali-
ciously and infamously conspire together in
order to injure the plaintiff." Notwithstanding the prejudices and opposition there was
against him, Hopkins did not lose the confidence or respect of the citizens of the state

[1] Hopkins Papers, vol. 3, page 14.

[2] *Ibid.*

by this action of Congress and the findings
of a jury of his peers. If he had been the
unprincipled person that has been pictured
he would soon have disappeared from the
stage of public life and never more have been
heard of; public sentiment does not uphold
such men; but the situation was well understood by the people of the state. They knew
that he was being persecuted by a set of men
whose influence was so powerful that it was
wiser to disregard it than to antagonize it,
and they kept their own counsel. Congress
had revenged itself on the man who had
spoken carelessly of it, and Hopkins had
been told by twelve of his fellow men that
no injury to his reputation or character had
accrued by reason of the allegations made
against him. Thus ended his troubles
brought about by his connection with the
American Navy, but it did not end his connection with the cause in which the colonies
were then desperately engaged. Public confidence in him was not lessened, and upon
retiring from his command he at once
enlisted heart and soul in the public service
in other fields of usefulness.

CHAPTER VII

IT was on the second day of January, 1778, that Hopkins was dismissed from the naval service of the United States, and a career which promised much at the outset came to an end.

It was not in his nature, however, to remain inactive. His enemies had triumphed, surely, but he was not without friends. His townsmen recognized his abilities and his patriotic motives too, and at the spring election following his dismissal from the naval service he was again elected a deputy to the General Assembly from the town of North Providence, which he represented from 1777 to 1786. The situation in Rhode Island during a portion of this period was most critical. The British forces held possession of Newport, and the lower bay was patrolled by British war vessels. Marauding parties from the enemy's camp frequently descended upon the bay side towns, and a state of warfare existed which kept the people constantly on the alert. and the militia of the state continually u n d e r arms.

Soon a f t e r Hopkins took his seat in the legislature that body appointed h i m a m e m b e r of t h e Council of War, and this position he held during the entire period of its service.

During the years of the war he was frequently employed on various committees having the charge of military affairs. Particularly was he active on committees appointed to adjust the accounts of the several regiments of the state, and as late as 1791. some years after his services i n t h e legislature had terminated, he was appointed, with Benjamin Bourn, to examine and adjust the claim of General

Ezekiel Cornell for his services during the
years of the Revolutionary struggle. While
a member of the General Assembly, in 1785,
he was elected Collector of Imposts for the
county of Providence, and held this office for
one year.

It was in this year also that Hopkins'
distinguished brother, Stephen, closed his
career, full of years and honors. He had
been in public life for more than forty years,
and no man had attained a wider reputation
in the colonies than Stephen Hopkins of
Rhode Island.[1] His influence was powerful
from the very beginning of the struggle for
American Independence. Of all the delegates in the Continental Congress none inspired greater respect, was so closely followed
in debate or was so highly valued for his
opinions as Stephen Hopkins; yet, after he
had left that body, and at the moment when
all these influences were so necessary to the
future of Esek Hopkins, he was powerless to
extend any assistance. Esek Hopkins undoubtedly owed much to the influence of his
brother, not only in official preferment but

[1] For an exhaustive study of his life and character see "Stephen
Hopkins, a Rhode Island Statesman, by William E. Foster,
Providence, Sidney S. Rider, 1884."

in the example set of patriotic duty to his
country and unselfish service to his fellow
men.

It was his privilege during the last year
of his service in the legislature to nominate
the Rev. James Manning to represent Rhode
Island in the Continental Congress, and he
was elected to that body, where he served
one year. Manning at this time was president of Rhode Island College, and the
two men had strong attachments for each
other.

Esek Hopkins had attained the ripe age
of seventy-three years before his public
career terminated. For more than thirty
years he had served in various public
stations, and the regularity with which he
had been chosen to represent his town and
state is the strongest evidence of his ability,
honesty and integrity in all his dealings.

Not only had he been called upon to give
of his talents and his time in managing the
affairs of government of the state of his birth,
but his wise counsel had been recognized by
the institution of learning which had been
established in Providence a few years before,
and in 1782 he was elected one of the trus-
tees of Rhode Island college, afterwards

Brown University, which position he held at
the time of his death. Among the students
in the college, graduating in the class of
1787, was Jonathan Maxey, a young man
from Attleboro, Mass. The same year
Maxey became a tutor in the university,
and served until 1791, when he was chosen
pastor of the First Baptist Church, and in
August of that year married Hopkins'
daughter, Susannah. He subsequently was
elected president of the college and had a
distinguished career.

Heart Hopkins, another daughter, was a
woman of great culture, and, quite in advance of the period, took the regular course
of study at the college, under the special
direction of her brother-in-law, its president.

About this time the afflictions of old age
began to creep upon Hopkins; he partially
lost the use of his limbs in "consequence of
a paralytic stroke," so that he was obliged
to go about on crutches. On the fifth of
December, 1796, he was still further afflicted
by the death of his oldest son, Captain John
Burroughs Hopkins, who had served so gal-
lantly with him in the Navy.

Connected with the feebleness of old age

16

there is an incident so touching that it arouses our sympathies and brings vividly before us the heart aches and sufferings of this venerable man. It will be remembered that during the proceedings in Congress against Hopkins no one took so firm a stand in his defence as did John Adams. We recall the scene between William Ellery and Adams when, at the close of the debate, Ellery advanced to the seat of Adams, and, giving him his hand, thanked him for his final plea in behalf of the Commander, and also said: "You have made the old man your friend for life; he will hear of your defence of him and he never forgets a kindness."

Years went by, and Adams was called to the highest office in the gift of the people of the new nation. No one watched his advancement with greater interest or felt a deeper pride and satisfaction than Esek Hopkins. To him Adams stood out distinct and apart from all other men in the whole land, the embodiment of manliness and honesty. In the time of adversity he had been Hopkins' friend; not such a friend as is secured by the enthusiasm of political strife, but a friend, earnest and sincere, deter-

HOME OF USER HOPKINS.

mined to know the truth and base his whole judgment upon it. In the summer of 1797 John Adams, with his family, stopped in Providence on his way to his Massachusetts home. It was the first opportunity that had been offered to the citizens of the town to pay their respects to him since he had been elected to the presidency, and great preparations were made to honor the distinguished guest. The president was escorted into the town by the Providence Light Dragoons, a company which had been formed some years before, and his arrival was signalled by the ringing of bells and the roar of cannon. He was escorted to the Golden Ball tavern, where accommodations had been provided for himself and family. "In the evening the College edifice and some private dwellings were brilliantly illuminated" and the whole town put on a gala appearance. That night, while the president was resting in his room with his family, he was informed that a gentleman wished to see him. Leaving them he went to one of the waiting rooms and there found an old man bowed with years and infirmities. It was Esek Hopkins. In his feeble condition he had been driven to the inn that he might show his respect and express his gratitude to the man who, years before, had stood up for him in the hour of trouble. Propped up by his crutches, his eyes overflowing with tears and his heart filled with emotion, he thanked the president for his interest taken in defending him from the attacks of his enemies.

This episode made a deep impression upon Adams, and he detailed the occurrence in the diary of the events of that journey, and afterwards wrote as he recalled the pathetic scene that Hopkins said: "he knew not for what end he was continued in life, unless it were to punish his friends or teach his children and grandchildren to respect me," and Adams further adds: "The president of Rhode Island College who had married his (Hopkins) daughter and all his family showed me the same affectionate attachment."

There was a social side to Esek Hopkins' character that was as pronounced as it was interesting and attractive. He was fond of the companionship of young people, and at all social functions of his friends and neighbors he was a conspicuous figure. He is said to have danced well, was bright and entertaining in conversation, and his company was always enjoyed on account of all these attractive qualities. No party, ball, or similar gathering was thought to be complete without his presence, and only when important engagements or ill health prevented did he fail to be numbered among the guests. As he advanced in years, and sickness prevented him from taking part in any such pleasures, it became a source of much disappointment to him. For a long time previous to his death he was confined to his bed, unable to move, yet possessed of all his faculties and exhibiting a keen interest in all that was going on about him.

The last days of his life were attended with much suffering, yet he calmly awaited the end with marked patience and quiet resignation. On the evening of Friday, February 26, 1802, the long and useful life of this venerable man came to an end. On the following Tuesday (March 2) his body was borne to the little God's Acre on the homestead farm, followed by a large number of "affectionate relatives and friends."

His death was mourned by the people of the state, to whom he had become endeared by his years of active public service. Some idea of the estimation in which he was held by his fellow men may be derived from the following announcement of his death, published in the *Providence Gazette*, on March 6, 1802:

"On Friday the 26th ult. at his residence in North Providence, Esek Hopkins, Esq.; in the 84th year of his age. His remains were on Tuesday last followed to the grave by a respectable concourse of affectionate relatives and friends. Through the different stages of a long life, the character of this gentleman was uniformly distinguished by an energetic mind, and a steadiness of principle, which age and infirmity were unable to impair. A genuine fortitude of mind, a lively sensibility of heart, and an immovable adherence to integrity were his general characteristics. With patience and resignation he continued to sustain the afflictions of disease, till he calmly resigned his life, while the agonies of death could not extort a groan. In him his children have lost an affectionate parent, society a worthy member and his country an inflexible patriot. In the American Revolution, he stood forth in the perils and hardships of war. He was honored with the command of the first naval expedition equipped by the Continental Congress, and was the first who dared to unfurl the American

flag in defiance of a powerful foe. The
duties of many important offices were by his
fellow citizens confided to him, of which he
acquitted himself with reputation and ability.
In the Legislature of the State he long sustained a seat, and was a member thereof at
the time of the adoption of the federal consti-
tution, which he then strenuously advocated,
and has uniformly continued to support."

Of the ten children[1] born to Esek and
Desire Hopkins, five were sons and five
daughters; all of his sons died before him,
while all the daughters survived their father.

On the fifteenth of September previous to
his death Hopkins executed his will, gener-
ously remembering his children and grandchildren and amply providing for their future
welfare. He left little personal estate, which
consisted mostly of household furniture, cattle

---

[1] The ten children of Esek and Desire Hopkins were :

John Burroughs Hopkins, b. Aug. 25, 1742 ; d. Dec. 5, 1776.
Heart, b. Sept. 1, 1744; d. July 11, 1825.
Abigail, b. Oct. 25, 1746; d. April 25, 1821.
Samuel, b. Feby. 19, 1748; d. Sept. 22, 1750.
Amey, b. Jan. 26, 1751; d. Dec. 14, 1835.
Stephen, b. March 6, 1753; d. July 3 1761.
Susanna, b. May 19, 1756; d. ——— 1803.
Esek, b. June 9, 1758; d. ——— 1777.
Samuel, b. ——— d. Dec. 1782.
Desire, b. May 17, 1764; d. May 20, 1843.

and farm implements, but his holdings of real
estate covered more than two hundred acres
in the neighborhood of his homestead. To
his three daughters, Heart, Desire and
Susanna, he bequeathed the mansion house
where he had lived so long. This house is
situated in Providence on Admiral street,
named in Hopkins' honor many years ago.
It still remains in the possession of one of
his descendants, being now owned by Mrs.
Frederick L. Gould, of Cambridge, Massachusetts, a great great granddaughter.

Originally it was a two story gambrel roof
house, not an elaborate or imposing struc-
ture, but from time to time additions have
been made until now it is full of quaint cor-
ners and little ells. The old well, with its
substantial well house in the rear of the
kitchen, yet supplies water for the household
as clear and sparkling as it was when Esek
Hopkins first came there to dwell. Nearly a
mile away to the northward is the graveyard
where the remains of the distinguished Commander lie buried with others of his kindred.
This tract of land, or as it was called, " the
burying place," was conveyed' to the town

¹ Pawtucket Record of Deeds, Book 2, page 377.

HOME OF ESEK HOPKINS.

Interior, Library

of North Providence by Esek Hopkins, on
September 20, 1791, "for a burying place
for that use only." When a part of North
Providence was annexed to the city of
Providence this burying ground was brought
within the city limits and is now known as
" Hopkins' Park," proceedings having been
taken by the municipality towards this end.
A bronze figure, heroic size, has been reared
over his grave through the liberality of a de-
scendant¹ and the municipality, representing
the Commander in his uniform of the navy.
On the pedestal is inscribed this legend, prepared by the author of this work :

ESEK HOPKINS

COMMANDER IN CHIEF

OF THE

CONTINENTAL NAVY

DURING THE

AMERICAN REVOLUTION

FROM DEC 22 1775 TO JAN 2 1778

BORN APRIL 26 1718 DIED FEB 26 1802.

¹ The late Harriet N. H. Coggeshall

It is doubtful if there was any more experienced seaman or skillful navigator to be
found in any of the colonies at the outbreak
of the American Revolution than Esek Hopkins. He was then a man of mature years,
had commanded ships for more than thirty
years, comprising merchantmen and privateers. and no American ship master was
better known in foreign parts. It is not
too much to say that there were other ship
masters who possessed similar capabilities,
were skillful navigators and brave seamen.
It was not these qualifications alone that
caused Esek Hopkins to be selected to
command the navy of the united colonies.

The material from which to select such a
commander and even officers for a navy list
was scant indeed. With the organization of
a naval service a new system and order from
that hitherto in vogue on vessels was demanded. a discipline strict. almost severe, was
imperative.

The ship master of that period, as now,
was an autocrat on board his vessel, but there
was little distinction between the relationship
of officers and men. The forecastle and
quarter-deck mingled in the most friendly
manner.

The officers and seamen were intimate friends, neighbors, or associates at home, and on ship board continued the intimacy. There was a discipline peculiar to the sea which was firm and unyielding, but it was not such as was expected on a government ship.

When a navy was projected this element in its composition was a subject of much concern; the colonies never had carried on naval affairs to any extent. A certain experience might have been had by the men who had served on the colony coast guard ships, but the life on these quasi government vessels was more free and easy, if any thing, than that aboard the merchantmen and privateers.

Even with the military forces in the colonies the same difficulty existed only to a lesser degree. From the earliest days of the settlements in America a military force had been essential to the life of the colonists.

Trainings had been instituted, and were followed up with strict regularity; a certain proficiency in tactics and discipline had been accomplished, and even some active experience in the field had been obtained in the Colonial wars. But with even this experience, when the military force of the

colonies was called into the field there was
a decided lack of military methods. Discipline, too, was lax, the officers were selected
with due regard to their experience and
capabilities, but the fact that they were
popular with the men and companionable
fellows had great weight in securing their
appointments. This relationship was continued in the camp and field, and officers and
men met on a common level. This being
the state of the military force, with years of
organization, it was important that in organ-
izing a naval force that some one skilled as
a master mariner and possessed of a sufficient knowledge of discipline and the government of a body of men should be selected.

Of all the available men for the command
of the navy, none, it was considered, combined so many qualifications as Esek Hopkins; at the moment of his selection he was
in command of a brigade of militia and conducting delicate negotiations with the enemy.
His appointment to the position was a distinguished honor, but it was an honor which
it would have been far better for him to have
refused, and accepted one less important.
His lack of success in the position was not
entirely owing to himself; he was a victim of

circumstances, but he lacked certain essential qualities that constitute a commander.

Cooper has well said: " There was no lack of competent navigators, or of brave seamen, but the high moral qualities which are indispensable to the accomplished officer, are hardly to be expected among those who have received all their training in the rude and imperfect school of the merchant service."

At this period there was no regularity of system and no standard of discipline in the navy. " The irregularities of the service, it is true," says Cooper, " grew out of the exigencies of the times, but their evils were incalculable. Rank, that great source of contention in all services in which it is not clearly defined and rigidly regulated, appears to have created endless heart burnings. The dissensions of the officers, naturally communicated themselves to the men; and, in time, this difficulty was added to the others which existed in obtaining crews." " They are jealous of him" alleged Chaplain Reed, in his complaint against Hopkins to the Marine Committee, and he sounded the key note in the whole miserable plot when he subscribed his name to these words. Combined with the jealousy of the officers in the fleet, and

the revengeful spirit that pervaded the minds
of those men outside, together with the petty
politics that pervaded the Continental Congress during the earlier period of the war,
there was fuel enough to start a fire which
no one could tell what it would consume
before it was quenched.

The moral status of the navy in its early
days undoubtedly was not of the highest.
The rules of the service provided for a
chaplain, but it was not until long after the
navy was organized that such an officer was
enrolled. The first to be appointed was
John Reed, and he seems to have been more
willing to lend his influence to underhand
methods against his superiors than to pur-
sue a course more in keeping with his pro-
fession. Some light is thrown upon this
condition of the navy and the character of
the men who were so fearful of the "strange
oaths" of the Commander, by the following
letter which Hopkins wrote to the Reverend
Samuel Hopkins, of Newport:

"I received yours of the 26th September
yesterday, and am very much obliged to you
for your address and advice; and as to your
complaints of the people belonging to the
navy, I am now to let you know that I did

not enter into the navy as a divine and that
I am not qualified to act or give directions
in that matter. The Congress whom I serve,
made provision for a chaplain to perform
that necessary duty, but to my mortification
I have not been able to get a single man to
act in that character, although I have applied
to many. If you know of any one that has
the good will of mankind at heart sufficiently
to expose himself to necessary danger of that
service, should be glad if you would send
him, who you may depend will be treated
with due respect: and if none can be procured, I cannot but condole with you the
depravity of the times."

This letter, too, shows in a measure a condition which, it cannot be denied, was all too
conspicuous in the service during the period
of which I write. There was not that "high
feeling of personal pride and self respect that
create an *esprit de corps* and the moral courage and lofty sentiments that come in time
to teach the trained officer to believe any
misfortune preferable to professional disgrace." No more brave, patriotic, and skillful body of men could be found in the colonies than those who formed the naval list,
but those highly essential qualities were

decidedly lacking, nor could they be expected; the fault was not altogether theirs,
it was a condition of the times.

There can be no doubt but that Hopkins
was reckless in his speech. The mariner of
that period was often more expressive than
polite in his conversation, and profanity on
ship board as well as elsewhere was not uncommon. In this connection I am reminded
of the story of the Scotch deacon who made
a voyage with one of the members of his
church, a bluff old sea captain. One day a
terrible storm came on and all hands were
called upon to work ship. In the excitement and danger of the moment this old
captain used certain language which greatly
astonished the good deacon. He, however,
said nothing, but when the ship, after a successful voyage, dropped anchor in her home
port, the deacon lost no time in reporting to
the elders the language which the captain
had used during the storm at sea. In due
time the captain was called before the church
and charged with profane language — the
deacon reporting what was said. This bluff
old sea-dog opened his eyes with astonish-
ment and replied: " Bless you, that wasn't
swearing! If I didn't talk that way in a

HOME OF ESEK HOPKINS

storm, the sailors would think I didn't
know my business." And it is related that
this argument secured an unanimous ac-
quittal. Hopkins no doubt had spoken
carelessly of the men who were controlling
the affairs of the navy, and it cannot be
denied that that exercise of authority was
often meddlesome and irritating if not disrespectful and insulting.

A careful examination of the charges and
depositions against him will show that there
is nothing in them that can be criticised except those alleged words of disrespect. But
an officer who so far forgets himself as to
use language disrespectful to his superiors
incurs a liability which may seriously affect
his whole future, and so it did with Hopkins.

This failing on the part of Hopkins
was used to great disadvantage to him. It
furnished excellent material for his enemies
to base their attacks upon, and, in the hands
of the men who were behind this whole
miserable conspiracy, was used with telling
effect. There certainly is a vein of humor
in the statements made by these petty officers that "we know him to be one principal
obstacle or reason why this ship (*Warren*)
is not manned & people are afraid to engage

in the fleet through fear of their being turned
over to this ship." The idea of sailors being
afraid to ship aboard of a vessel whose commander used strong language is a unique
one in marine circles. Hopkins never was
charged with the abuse of his men; he abused
himself the most, and if there had been the
slightest grounds for this charge they would
have certainly taken advantage of such a
condition.

In his encounter with the stranded frigate
"*Diamond*" there appears little to criticise,
except, perhaps, his attempting an attack on
her in a small sloop, which was a piece of
bravado more censurable than his neglect to
do so with his ships. Below the "*Diamond*,"
not more than six or seven miles distant, was
a fleet of British war vessels riding at anchor
in Newport harbor; almost under the guns
of the "*Diamond*" was another English vessel riding on the water with her "anchor
a peak." With a strong west wind it would
have been possible for the British fleet, upon
receiving a signal from the vessel lying near
Patience Island, to have got under weigh
and arrived at the scene of action long before
the American ships lying up the river could
have found their way through the tortuous

channel southward in the face of this strong westerly gale. The "*Diamond*" was as safe from the attacks of the American vessels, even though she was stranded on an island in the bay, as she would have been in Newport harbor under the guns of the whole British fleet.

It was an easy matter to charge him with neglecting to capture a stranded vessel, but when the circumstances are taken into consideration it will be seen that however much Hopkins might have desired to accomplish this, there was no hope of doing so with the prevailing wind. But there are grounds for the belief that the stranding of the "*Diamond*," almost under the guns of a sister frigate, was but a ruse to lure Hopkins with his ships down the river, when a superior force of the enemy would suddenly appear and destroy them before they could beat up the winding channel to a safe anchorage at Providence.

No one knew his limitations better than Hopkins did himself. Repeatedly we find him writing to his brother and others in Congress: "Whenever you or the Congress think you can get a man in my room that will be of more service to the cause than I

can you have my leave, and in justice to the
Country I think you ought to do it;" at
another time he pleaded his years.

If he had promptly resigned his command
he might have avoided the complications
which ensued, but such would have been
cowardly, and no such impulse found a place
in his heart. He knew that he was becoming entangled in difficulties, and that there
was little hope for him to escape, yet he had
pledged his life and his honor in a cause
which he loved and to which he was devoted,
and if, in the struggle, he fell, it would be in
the discharge of his duty.

On the twenty-fourth of June, 1865, the
town of North Providence celebrated the
one hundreth anniversary of its corporate
existence. On this occasion the Reverend
Massena Goodrich delivered a scholarly historical address, in which he referred to the
men of the town who had achieved eminence
in the nation's history, and used these words
—a fitting tribute to a loyal son: " Of those
whose homes were in this town, and who did
bold service during the Revolutionary war,
the name of Commodore Hopkins stands
eminent. Though born in another town,
he made for years this place his abode, and

his ashes are mouldering within its borders.
It were superfluous to praise him. His
valor is a part of the heroic heritage of his
native State. His name and Perry's, who
alike, in different wars, upheld the honor of
our country on the sea, have given our little
commonwealth cause to glory in her naval
warriors. For between two and three years
Hopkins was commander-in-chief of the navy,
but the bitter sectional feeling in Congress,
which operated so much on many an occasion to the disparagement of New England
men, finally succeeded in ousting him from
his honorable position. But by this act our
country suffered most."

APPENDIX

PORTRAITS OF ESEK HOPKINS.

There are seven known portraits of Esek Hopkins,
the earliest being included in a group painted by
John Greenwood, about the year 1770, and is probably the only life portrait extant. A full description of
this painting, and the circumstances under which it
was painted, will be found, with a photogravure repro-
duction of it, at page 28.

A mezzotint portrait of Hopkins, published in London, by Thomas Hart, Esq., August 22, 1776,
bearing the title "Commodore Hopkins Commander
in chief of the American Fleet Publish'd as the act
directs 22 Aug 1776 by Thos Hart," is the best known
of the Hopkins portraits, and has frequently been
copied. This portrait was evidently produced to
satisfy the demand for a likeness of the person who
had so suddenly sprung into fame, for Hopkins had
already become a naval hero. It is quite likely an
imaginary picture, for Hopkins could not have been
in London, or in England for that matter, for more
than a year previous to its publication, and previous
to this time he would have attracted no more attention than a hundred other sea captains. General
Henry Knox pictures Hopkins' appearance within
a few weeks of the time when the Hart portrait was
published, and describes him as "an antiquated figure"
(see page 134), which the portrait does not confirm.

The author ventures the opinion that but few of the engraved portraits of celebrities of the Revolution were likenesses of the person they purported to portray. They were produced to satify a popular demand. As evidence of this compare this Portrait Plate 1 with the following in "Narrative and Critical History of America," Winsor, Vol. VI.

Israel Putnam, page 192, which is reproduced from an engraving published by C. Shepard, 9 September, 1775, probably in London.

Benedict Arnold, page 223; a mezzotint of this was published in London, in 1776, the same year as the Hart mezzotint.

Benedict Arnold, page 448; this appears in "Geschichte der Kriege, in und ausser Europa, Eilfter Theil, Nürnberg, 1778." Compare also with Portrait Plate 2, John Sullivan, page 637; this was also published in London, August 22, 1776, from which the copy in "Geschichte der Kriege" is made.

A print bearing the title "Commodore Hopkins Commander en chef der Armej : Flotte" Portrait Plate 2 is in "Geschichte der Kriege," 1778; it is evidently copied from the Hart portrait with material changes in the background.

A rare print is in possession of the Rhode Island Historical Society, volume of portraits, page 90, a copy of which is Portrait Plate 3. This is also the Hart portrait, without the background of ships. It is inscribed " Hopkins Commandant en chef la flotte Americaine." Beneath the ellipse, within which is the portrait, are representations of the two flags associated with early Revolutionary history, the one bearing the injunction " Don't tread upon me," the other, " Liberty Tree. An appeal to God ; " scrolls,

palms, laurels, liberty cap, cannon and other acces-
sories, form a fanciful border for the portrait. No
information is obtained relative to the origin of this
portrait.

Winsor, in "Narrative and Critical History of
America, Vol. VI, page 570, note," mentions a portrait in " Nederlandsch Mercurius," XXIII, page 128.
An extended search has failed to disclose a copy of
this periodical. Portrait Plate 3 may be this Dutch
portrait. If not, then another is added to this interesting collection of Hopkins' portraits.

A far different portrait of Hopkins from these is
in "Murray's Impartial History of the American
War" (Vol. 11), a copy of which is Portrait Plate 4 :
it bears the title "Commodore Hopkins." It was
engraved for "Murray's History of the American
War," by R. Pollard, and "Printed for T. Robson
New Castle upon Tyne." Mr. Pollard is probably
responsible for the features depicted.

A ludicrous full length portrait accompanies "An
Impartial History of the War in America between
Great Britain and her Colonies from its commencement to the end of the year 1779;" London, printed
for R. Faulder, New Bond street, MDCCLXXX.
This portrait bears the title " Robert Hopkins, Commodore of the American Sea Forces." A story of
Hopkin's life is contained in this volume which doubtless originated in the brain of the author of it. All
therein contained may, however, have happened to
Robert Hopkins, whoever he may have been, but
certainly it does not refer to Esek Hopkins. This
story is contained in Admiral Preble's " Esek Hopkins" in the *United Service, Feby., 1885*. Portrait
Plate 5 is a copy of this.

An oil portrait of Hopkins is in Sayles' Memorial Hall, Brown University, Providence, painted by Thomas J. Heade. It was copied in the early part of the present century from the Hart mezzotint. Heade was a painter of renown in Providence, and numerous portraits testify to his ability and professional skill. A copy of this, Portrait Plate 6, is used as a frontispiece to this work.

INDEX

INDEX

— —

New York, 127, 135, 136, 143, 155, 186, 197.
Nicholas, Capt., 113, 115.
Nightingale, Joseph, 146.
Nightingale, Samuel Jr., 41, 43
North Carolina, 77, 95, 156, 164, 165.
North Providence, incorporated, 27.
Nova Scotia, 177.

Olney, Joseph, 9, 80, 109, 223
Orders to Commander-in-Chief, 84.
   to Captain Stone, 91.
Origin of American Navy, 69.
Origin of names of vessels, 82.
Osborn, William, 137.
Otway, Lieutenant, 203.
Owen, Captain, 26.
Oyster Bay, 4.

Page, Ambrose, Capt., 28, 30, 41, 43, 223 228.
Paine, Robert Treat, 72
   Thomas, 183
Parker, Sir Peter, 190.
Patience Island, 172, 258.
Patrick, John, 138.
Pearce, Benoni, 13.
Peck, George, 110.
Penobscot, 178.
Perry, 261.
Petition to Congress against Hopkins, 187, 188, 189.
Philadelphia, 69, 77, 95, 104, 126, 130 133, 136, 137, 152, 153, 154, 159, 162, 191, 195, 202, 204, 224, 225
Pierce, William, 106.
Pinkney, Charles C., 88, 89
   Thomas, 88.
Pitcher, Jonathan, 20, 107, 207.
Plymouth, 208.
Pollard, R., 267.
" Polly," a sloop, 57.
Pony, Jacob, 138.
Pope, 76.
Potter, Richard, 108.

Potter, Stephen, 223, 230.
   William 37,
Powder scarcity of, 104.
   sent away, 117.
Powell, Colonel, 89.
Powel, James, 107
Power, Nicholas, 29, 41.
Preble, Admiral, 267.
Privateers interfere with the manning of the fleet, 145
" Providence," 81, 108, 122, 133, 135, 136, 147, 161, 169, 171 172, 175, 178 179, 198, 200, 203, 207 208, 228.
Providence Gazette, 47, 246.
Putnam, Israel, 266.

Quebec, 110.
Queen Anne, 112.

Randall, Stephen, 6.
Randolph, Peyton, 72
Rathbun, John, 108.
Ravencroft, Joseph, 138.
Rawson, Elizabeth, 207
Read, Joseph, Colonel, 208.
Reding, Lewis, 138.
Reed, John, 181, 186, 188, 189, 191, 192, 197, 204, 205, 206, 222 253 254.
Reiney, Christopher, 138.
Revolution, first naval fight, 66.
Reynolds, William, 108.
Rhode Island College, 10, 244.
Richards, Peter, 108.
Rider, Sidney S., 239
Roatch, John, 138
Roberts, David, 108.
   Owen, 88
Robinson, Robert, 106.
Robson, T., 267.
Rogers, 109.
Rogers, Woodes, 111, 112.
Rome, George, 53.
" Rose," a brig, 27.
" Rose," frigate, 40, 47, 64.
Round Robin, petition for pay, 137.
Rules of the Fox Point battery, 41.

www.ingramcontent.com/pod-product-compliance
Lightning Source LLC
Chambersburg PA
CBHW030925050726
47498CB00003BA/900